CW00531275

The Book of Indian Ghosts

The munchowa, a ghost found in Kanpur

CONTENTS

The Book of Indian Ghosts

Riksundar Banerjee

Illustrations by
Raka Chowdhury

ALEPH

ALEPH

ALEPH BOOK COMPANY
An independent publishing firm
promoted by *Rupa Publications India*

First published in India in 2021
by Aleph Book Company
7/16 Ansari Road, Daryaganj
New Delhi 110 002

ISBN: 978-93-90652-26-6

3 5 7 9 10 8 6 4 2

Printed at Sanat Printers

INTRODUCTION

There are more things in Heaven and Earth,
Horatio, than are dreamt of in your Philosophy.
—William Shakespeare, *Hamlet.*

In the history of time, one lifespan disappears like a pebble in the sea. What happens after we die? Do we leave this existence forever? For millennia, the fear of the unknown has inspired a deep fascination about the afterlife among humans. This fascination is usually tinged with dread, although, the idea of an eternity spent wallowing in misery doesn't make much sense. Be that as it may, this fear of the unknowable eternity that awaits us after we leave our earthly shells is what has given rise to the concept of ghosts.

Fear is a powerful emotion. It is born out of our psychological interpretations of day-to-day experiences. Upon analysis, the source of almost all our fears can be traced to that of the unknown. Whenever we come across a phenomenon which cannot be explained by our existing knowledge and experiences, we feel overwhelmed with fear. Religious beliefs provide an optimistic overview of an afterlife in some form of 'heaven' or 'hell' depending on our mortal deeds. Yet, every concept that has been advanced from time immemorial is hypothetical, leaving room for imagination to spread its wings. Thus, stories of ghosts, which surround our mortal existence, become a way of confronting the unknown.

Do ghosts exist? Around the world, there are endless studies and discussions on this subject. Simply put, ghosts are lifeless beings that inspire fear. Sometimes they are the spirit of someone who was once alive. Other times, they simply fall beyond the physical rules of the universe. These uncanny beings have found mention in primeval epics like the Ramayana or Mahabharata; *Tanakh*, the Hebrew Bible; *The Egyptian Book of the Dead*; the *Iliad*; and the *Odyssey*, among others.

Ghost lore has been part of the popular imagination. Around the fifth century BCE, a physical projection of ghosts was staged in the classical Greek drama *Oresteia* by Aeschylus. During the European Renaissance, a book called *Of Ghostes and Spirites, Walking by Night* by Ludwig Lavater was said to have been reprinted several times. The mythical *One Thousand and One Nights* also includes tales of supernatural beings.

Later, around 1173 AD, the Dracula called Count Estruch became very popular and terrifying. According to Catalan mythology, Count Estruch died fighting against witchcraft. The practice of witchcraft was prevalent in medieval Britain. Agnes, also known as the Wise Wife of Keith, was said to be one of the witches who terrorized East Lothian of Scotland during the North Berwick Witch Trials, 1590[*]. Later, the Brown Lady of Raynham

---

[*]Thomas Thomson, *The Historie and Life of King James the Sext*, Edinburgh, 1825, p. 241.

Hall became one of the most famous hauntings of spooky Britain since the photographers from *Country Life* magazine claimed to have captured an image of this lady in 1835.[*]

Elsewhere in Europe, the concept of the vampire, that still creates a sensation among writers and filmmakers, was first introduced in Hungary. The German spirit poltergeist, which creates a racket and moves objects with loud noise, found its place in many modern cinematic representations. The banshee, an Irish spirit, was said to have made its ghastly appearance just before deaths in families. A widespread myth of the monster called the goblin could be found all across Europe, during the Middle Ages. This mischievous creature had a small, hairy body with a greed for gold, and sometimes possessed magical abilities as well.

Another very popular concept of ghosts called the zombie, first originated in Haitian folklore. Zombies are supposed to be magically resurrected human corpses which have an insatiable appetite for fresh flesh.

When it comes to Indian mythical ghosts, these are to be found in ancient Indian sacred texts like the Rigveda, where a classification of ghosts can be found. More of these mythical creatures found in Indian history are described here in this book.

Literature, movies, drama, paintings, etc., have always played significant roles in representing social structures. Remarkably, in all of these genres, ghosts or spiritual beings have marked their presence in some way. Naturally, their characteristics are influenced by the geographic, cultural, and temporal spaces in which they are brought to life, so to say. Yet, there are strange similarities between

---

[*]*Country Life Magazine*, 26 December 1936.

all these ghosts regardless of which part of the world they belong to.

The definition of 'class' has evolved over time. During the medieval period, this classification was based on the occupational role assigned to an individual in society. As a result, ancient tales often placed supernatural beings within the folds of the prevalent social hierarchy in a sort of mirror image, or perhaps ghost image. This is why, there is a definitive hierarchy in the supernatural world with monsters, demons, pretas, rakshasas or spirits, taking their places alongside humans and gods. A detailed exploration of this aspect of the spirit world is beyond the scope of this book but it is definitely something worth mentioning.

Over time, humans realized that the dead would always outnumber the living. The void created by the absence of someone is impossible to fill. But the discomfort and ambiguity that follow death emerge in the tales of the deceased who return among us as ghosts. There are numerous possible reasons why these otherworldly figures enter the imagination of the living. For example, someone who had been oppressed in their lifetime might come back to seek justice. Throughout history, there have been brutal injustices perpetrated on those belonging to the marginalized sections of the society. This may have led to the emergence of legends about notorious spirits such as the masan or kanipishachi that notably set about seeking justice for their oppressed 'class'. Significantly, the dayani of North India seeks to avenge the brutality meted out to lower-caste, dark-skinned women. The oppression and pain of women throughout centuries have engendered one of the largest corpuses of ghost stories. It explains why there are so many female ghosts in both literature and film. Throughout history, in all cultures, women have been deprived, tortured, and victimized. Other than the patriarchy, social barriers have also heavily affected women. In Indian culture, there was a time (until the eighteenth century) when a man could have a large number of wives. The chief role of these wives was to keep giving birth until their bodies eventually gave up. Naturally, there are innumerable stories that can be found of ghosts that have risen from the death of pregnant women, or women who died while giving birth, or women who were sexually abused, and so on. Whether it is the sankhchunni or the chiroguni—these blood-curdling ghosts seek revenge on behalf of women who were terrorized when they were alive. The legends surrounding the ghosts of unmarried women, such as the petni or the kichin, strike fear since they can also seek horrific sexual gratification from the living. Sexual desires have often driven ghosts into finding a way back to the mortal world. Even some male ghosts like the supurus have a reputation for attempting to have sex. Female spirits are not the only sort of ghosts who seek vengeance. In fact, the majority of unquiet phantoms are those who are seeking vengeance on those who oppressed or murdered them when they were living.

India has, arguably, the most diverse families of ghosts to be found anywhere on the planet because of the simple fact that Indian society is, arguably, the most diverse on earth, with each of its subsets having a distinctive method of worship, culture, lifestyle, and so on. As with the mortal world, so with the spirit world. Most of the communities in our society have their own types of ghouls, spirits, and other undead creatures. However, a number of them have several things in common, should not be surprising given that all Indians have a fair amount in common. An interesting fact of the spirit world is that spectres are but a reflection of the society they arise from. When calm, peace, equality, and fraternity become the traits most associated with our society, all malevolent spirits will drift away. The answer to our nightmares lies within us.

This book is by no means exhaustive but does include a representative sample of ghosts from every part of the country. In the course of my years of research, I found a lot of material about ghosts in published literature but the most interesting material I found was in oral tales of the spirit world. The illustrations featured in this book are improvisations of existing sketches that I came across during the course of my research. Some of them were drawn from scratch according to the descriptions provided by the locals whom I had interviewed. The interesting sidelight that came up during my study of ghosts was the unevenly large number of ghosts I encountered in Bengali literature and culture. My findings could, of course, be attached to the fact that I am a Bengali and based in Bengal, and, therefore, had greater access and insight into Bengali culture, literature, and society. However, this may have also had to do with the Bengali history of violence in recent times, starting with the Battle of Plassey and its aftermath, in the eighteenth century, furthered by the origins of killing in the centuries that came after. Other parts of India, too, have experienced horrific violence over the years, and I'd be interested to hear from anyone who has researched the incidence of ghostly sightings and tales of the spirit world unique to these parts.

For this book, I have collected ghost stories from various sources—books on ghosts in the regional languages, especially in the Bengali language; I have also reimagined ghostly encounters that I first came across in books that I had bought from book fairs and read through the night when I was a child fascinated with otherworldly creatures and their worlds; from stories and folk tales narrated by locals to me in the course of my research. My enduring fascination with the spirit world eventually led me to do a PhD on the subject. And, from there, it was a natural progression to writing books on the subject. After a few works in Bengali, this is my first book in English. I hope it will give you a few chills and thrills.

Riksundar Banerjee
Kolkata
1 March 2021

1

AACHERI

'She is gone! She never came home....!'

Sobbing loudly, Tamang was standing on the veranda of Mr Paul's bungalow. He had just returned from a trip to his village. When he came back, he couldn't find his daughter in the fields. His wife, too, had not returned from the tea garden where she worked during the day.

Mr Paul was the manager of a tea estate in Sikkim. Initially sceptical of taking a job far away from his home in Kolkata, he had been swayed by the blue mountains of northern Sikkim, its unhurried lifestyle, and the generous amenities of the tea estate. He had many people to take care of his meals and other household chores. He was so well taken care of that he didn't even feel the need to shift his family from Kolkata.

Tamang, the watchman of the bungalow, lived on the tea estate with his wife and daughter. His daughter used to play in the bungalow courtyard in the evenings. Mr Paul would sometimes watch her play with the wildflowers that she had collected on her way back from school while singing a melancholic song in her native tongue. He could only remember the first two words of the song, 'pheri bhetaula'.

It wasn't unusual for people to go missing in these areas. But most times, they would come back from the missed turn that took them into the wilderness. Despite the perilous terrain and wild animals, they would find their way back. Tamang's wife had last been seen leaving work early, but she never picked up her daughter from school. People searched everywhere for days, scoured all the possible routes she could have taken on her way back from work, but all in vain. Mr Paul tried to console Tamang, who, devastated, would spend his days sobbing in the garden and, at other times, staring blankly at the gardens from the backyard of the bungalow.

One day, Mr Paul woke up to a distant tune of music. A soft voice singing a folk song that echoed in the backyard. He ran to his window at once and saw Tamang sitting in the garden with a bunch of wildflowers in his lap. The moonlit mountains behind him grieved in silence and probably echoed the music back at him.

Even though his heart broke looking at this scene, he could swear he had heard a girl's voice. Gradually, this became a regular affair. Sometimes he could even make out the words 'pheri bhetaula' clearly but he could never trace the source of the song. Confused, he began thinking he was losing his wits. Once, Mr Paul even followed the sound that seemed to be coming from the bottom of the abyss and stopped right at the edge when he realized where he was going.

Overwhelmed, he decided to leave this godforsaken place and resigned from his job as quickly as possible. On the day he was leaving, he decided to say goodbye to Tamang.

'Well, goodbye, then,' he said awkwardly.

Tamang smiled weakly. 'Pheri bhetaula, sir.'

Mr Paul was startled. 'W–what does that mean?'

'It means "see you again". It's a common way of saying goodbye in Nepali, sir.'

Mr Paul couldn't bring himself to say anything further. He packed his bags and took the next train home.

This time around, the feverish crowd of Kolkata felt warm to him. His daughter was delighted to have him back, and he felt foolish for having left his family in the first place. His wife was so pleased she hosted a party, inviting all his childhood friends. It was a relaxing and fun–filled evening that temporarily wiped away the recent trauma that had filled his head. It felt wonderful to hear people laughing and singing on his rooftop garden. One of his friend's sons could play the guitar and played a bunch of songs for everyone. Before the last song, the boy said to Mr Paul's daughter, 'This one's for you, Aacheri! I'm so glad uncle gave you a Nepali name. They are a beautiful people.'

Mr Paul felt uneasy. When had he called his daughter Aacheri? He smiled awkwardly and waited for the song to end with his heart fluttering in his chest. He was somewhat relieved when the boy started a song called 'Resham Firiri', which everyone joined in chorus.

Later that night after everyone had left, he went looking for his daughter. The moment he stepped onto the terrace, he realized something was wrong. His daughter was lying on the floor, moaning and mumbling that her head hurt badly. Panicked, he shouted out to his wife who was downstairs. They took her to the hospital immediately, where she was taken into the intensive care unit and given sedatives.

Everything had happened so fast, Mr Paul felt exhausted after returning home that night. His wife too was bewildered and sat silently on the bed. Mr Paul realized this was the first time they were alone since he had come back. Unable to resist himself, he pulled her close and began to caress her. But his wife, feeling terrible about having sex while their daughter was in hospital, kept resisting. With great difficulty, she managed to shove him off.

'Is this what you did with her mother as well?' Mr Paul sat up with a jolt. His daughter was standing right beside the bed.

'She showed me what you did. Now I have seen it too! Is this what were you doing with her mother and her, Baba? Is this why she was shouting?'

Mr Paul felt chills run down his spine. He found himself rooted to the spot as he watched his daughter walk away from him to the balcony. She climbed over the railing.

'Her mother was sick and came home early from work. You didn't expect that, did you? So, you threw them both off the cliff! I saw it all. Even the way they fell. Do you want to see?' She leaned into thin air.

'Noooo!'

Stumbling, Mr Paul could no longer feel his legs as he ran towards his daughter. He didn't remember whether he tripped, or the girl pushed her, whether he was watching his daughter's face against the dark or those lovely pink cheeks that he couldn't get his hands off, whether he heard his own shout echoing from the bottom of the abyss or the screams of Tamang's wife and daughter.

Characteristics of the aacheri

- A child ghost.
- Haunts other children and makes them sick.
- When children die from a mishap or an accident in the mountains, their ghosts turn into aacheris.
- Kills people for revenge.
- Found mostly in the mountains of Sikkim.

2

AAYERI

Stephen was getting annoyed. His guide and the caretaker of the villa, Jimmy, had been accompanying him on all his ventures. In the beginning it had been helpful in order to familiarize himself with this obscure hill station. He had taken some great shots of the landscape and that was good enough as a cover. But Jimmy kept asking about his photographic interests and it was all getting a bit too much to deal with.

About a week later, he wondered whether this was just a coincidence or if Jimmy was keeping an eye on him. Paranoid, he'd hardly leave the house during the day. One afternoon Stephen pretended to be asleep. Jimmy came to the room, checked if he were sleeping and then went out to the market. Stephen quickly got up and left the villa through the back door with his huge backpack that he always kept ready. He knew his way around by now and kept going deeper into the forest that clothed the mountain. It had started getting dark and that was the best time for his purpose. He waited at the right spot until he spotted a fawn coming his way. He took aim and pulled the trigger.

It was difficult to skin the deer in the dark, but years of practice helped Stephen get his work done quickly. After storing the deerskin in his bag, he returned to the villa, where Jimmy was waiting for him. Standing at the backdoor, he quietly watched Stephen walk inside. Later that night, as Stephen was getting ready for bed, Jimmy came up to him and said, 'Please don't kill our animals, sir! I knew you were interested in hunting from the beginning. Every year, we see many poachers like you. But we protect our animals; please don't kill them.'

'Do you know how much money you could make if you were a bit smarter? There are so many rare animals in this part of the world. Do you know how much their skins sell for? Or the value of their horns?'

'It can't be more than their lives, sir,' Jimmy said and quickly left the room.

Stephen was fuming. The animals in this forest were among the rarest in the world. He was unable to understand how people could be so foolish and lose opportunities to profit from poaching them. He certainly wasn't going to miss his chance.

The next morning Stephen woke up to the sound of barking. When he came out into the backyard, he found Jimmy tying a dog to a post. He couldn't help chuckling at this feeble effort to stop him. He had poached leopards and bears, and these people thought they could stop him with a dog! Jimmy watched him calmly as he walked into the forest that afternoon.

This time, Stephen chose to go to the other side of the forest, which was quiet and dense. He chose his spot and waited with bated breath. It must have been his lucky day, for he spotted a red panda coming his way. Noiselessly, he aimed his gun at it.

Suddenly, a loud bark broke the silence of the forest. Startled, Stephen missed the shot. He looked up to realize the panda had scampered away. Infuriated, he pointed the gun in the direction of the barking and blasted off a shot. Years of practice on targeting sounds in the dark, he didn't miss the mark this time. The bark turned into a loud howl, followed by the quick steps of an animal and a human running away. With a satisfied smile, Stephen walked back, hoping these idiots had learnt their lessons by now.

Just then, he heard another bark. This time, reflexively, he pointed his gun towards the source. In the distance, he could see a human figure, surrounded by at least four or five dogs. In the shadowy light, he couldn't recognize the dogs, but by their raucous barks, they appeared to be full-sized hounds. Their viridescent eyes glowed in the dark, making the whole pack look even more terrifying.

The pack was slowly moving in Stephen's direction. Stephen grew very afraid but he kept his gun pointed unwaveringly at the pack of dogs barking occasionally. As they inched closer, he decided to take a shot at the dogs.

There was a dead silence after the shot. Barking madly now, the hounds moved faster. Standing still, Stephen shot again, and then again. This time he pointed his gun at the human with them and fired but that didn't stop the pack. Giving up, he started running deeper into the forest. He could hear the dogs running after him. He fired at the dogs rapidly but he couldn't outrun the hounds. The last thing he remembered was emerald green eyes closing in on him. Next to them was a man. Perhaps his eyes were glowing green as well....

Characteristics of the aayeri

- Takes the form of a man accompanied by a pack of dogs.
- Attacks hunters.
- When hunters die during a hunt, they are said to turn into the aayeri.
- Known to distract and scare hunters.
- Can be seen in the Himalaya.

3

ADAM BHEDIYA

Legends around werewolves exist in many shapes and forms. In India, the creature is called the adam bhediya. In myth and folklore, it is usually difficult to classify which origin story came first, although in this case, since the werewolf made its first appearance in European mythology in the Middle Ages, it can be surmised that the adam bhediya shares some of the characteristics of its western counterpart. The key reason could be geographical. Due to the warm weather, there are very few areas in India where werewolves survive. Naturally, the tales of these demons also gather around their natural residence, the spine-chilling hills of the Himalaya. Wolves are not traditionally the most menacing animals in India and include predators among their packs. Yet the mysterious nature of the adam bhediya, their indomitable physical bearings, have influenced blood-curdling tales about humans transforming into these feral beings.

The description and origin of the adam bhediya matches those of werewolves. It is believed that if someone was bitten or even scratched by one, they too would turn into an adam bhediya. Ordinarily, they possess human features. It is only on full-moon nights that they transform into ferocious monsters. As their whole body transforms into a huge wolf's, their teeth grow into fangs and fingernails into talons. The size of the body is believed to be much bigger than a human or a common wolf. On these nights, they gather immense power and hunt in the forests. Like wolves, they, too, howl and respond to other wolves.

If an adam bhediya attacks a human, they can devour them. If the human somehow manages to escape after being bitten, they also turn into an adam bhediya on full-moon nights. In their human form, they have no memories of their transformation on full-moon nights and vice versa. But the moment the full-moon period is over, they usually find themselves back in their human form lying somewhere in the middle of the forest. The next few days they are weakened and in pain. They are, however, believed to be just as dangerous on their human days since they can attack people around them. Gradually they stop being a part of the society and start dwelling in the forests even in human form. Myths also say that the humans who keep transforming into these violent creatures for a long time, start developing a harsh voice and cravings for flesh and blood even in their human form.

The adam bhediya can have a really long life. Whether immortal or not, it isn't clear how they can be hunted down. In every country where the tales of werewolves exist, there are believed to be distinct methods to tame or kill them. In India, it is believed that a stake made from the trees of their inhabiting forest has to be plunged into their heart to end the terror. Then the body has to be burnt immediately.

This comes as a terrible curse for normal human lives since a good person like the character of Professor Lupin in the *Harry Potter* books can also become a deadly monster every month and cause terrible agony for himself as well as for those around him.

Characteristics of the adam bhediya

- Similar to werewolves.
- Exists in the form of a normal human most of the time.
- Changes into a monstrous combination of half-human and half-wolf on full-moon nights.
- Is created when an adam bhediya bites a human being.

4

ATESWAR

Hiru and Biru were brothers who lived in a village in South Bengal. Their favourite festival was the festival of the ateswar ghost. On the day of the festival, not only were they free from school, they also got to eat loads of pitha, deep-fried sweet. The only drawback was that once the rituals were over, they had to throw away the pithas into the village pond. The brothers made sure they stocked up enough pithas for themselves before they were disposed of. They didn't bother with the rule that prohibited touching the sweets after the rituals. They couldn't understand why everybody worked so hard only to throw the delicious treats in the water.

As always, they sneaked into the kitchen in the afternoon, scooped up handfuls of pithas and, avoiding the adults, ran to the pond. Hiru, the elder one, had a feeling their mother knew what her boys were up to but kept quiet so that her sons could have more sweets than their cousins. They went to the pond since they knew it would be empty by the afternoon and, after everybody had finished taking their bath and daily ablutions, they could enjoy their feast in solitude.

Hiru gobbled up his portion while Biru took his time. This had always been the hardest part of sharing a meal between the brothers. Biru, a very slow eater, always had sweets left with him while Hiru, once done with his share, would fight his brother for more. Their mother would then intervene and scold Hiru. Today, Biru knew their mother would not come to his aid, so he was careful and hid his food from Hiru's watchful eyes. Hiru, on the other hand, had devised a plan to obtain Biru's sweets. He told his brother to take a dip in the pond so they could cool down. Since Hiru was a good swimmer, he dipped into the water and, popping his head above the surface of the water, started shouting: 'Hey, brother, look my body is gone!'

'What do you mean, Hiru?'

'It must be the ateswar. You know he only has a body and no head, right? He must have stolen my body as well. Can you get my body back, brother?'

'What should I do now?' Biru was on the verge of tears.

'Feed me some pithas. You know ateswars like pithas, he might give me back my body!'

Poor Biru was so scared, he broke into a run screaming at the top of his voice. Hiru, angry and dejected that his plan had failed, came out of the water and sat on the grass looking downcast. Biru would tell everyone about the stolen pithas, and he would lose his share from the evening meal as well. Now he would have to wait a whole year before he could eat his favourite sweet again. Depressed at the thought, Hiru looked ready to cry.

Suddenly, he felt a tap on his shoulder. He looked up to see a headless body standing before him, with water still dripping from the clothes. One of its hands was sticking out holding a variety of delectable pithas, many of which Hiru had never tried before.

Characteristics of the ateswar

- A water ghost with a headless body.
- Lives underwater.
- Not considered fatal. Can cause minor disturbances.
- Found in South Bengal.

5

BAGOWA BHOOT

Our eyes and ears often deceive us, but we tend to trust them more than we should. Often, what is in front of us is not what we perceive it to be.

There are innumerable kinds of superstitions and beliefs surrounding the paranormal world. The inhabitants of the Sundarbans delta, who eke out their living by harvesting honey from the beehives scattered in the depths of the jungle, believe in their local ghosts. The jungles are infested with tigers and crocodiles and the air is filled with the fishy smell of undead spirits lurking around.

A great number of these honey harvesters inevitably become fodder for the notorious man-eating Royal Bengal tigers. Many believe that the spirits of these people remain on earth until their mortal purpose is served. So, what happens after the tigers eat their bodies? Their spirits lie in wait in the form of the bagowa bhoot.

The bloodthirsty spirits roam the jungle, hunt down humans, creep into villages, and roar until the walls of huts tremble. They take the shape and form of the tiger that had killed them.

There are several stories about the bagowa bhoot in regional folklore. Here's one of them.

A man named Hiran went into the swamp with his fellow workers. When the group was taking down a beehive, Hiran went to collect dry wood for cooking. Absent-mindedly, he walked a bit further, when a faint smell of urine caught his attention. He realized that a tiger was nearby and that his life was in danger. Perfunctorily, he turned around and started running towards his group, but it was futile.

Nobody found any trace of Hiran. His wife became a baagh bidhaba, a tiger widow. As per societal diktats, she was left all on her own with her three hungry kids. Hiran's oldest son, Jamal, had to take up his father's job at a very early age. Jamal learned to collect wood and honey.

One day, the entire jungle burst into chaos: the birds were chirping, the monkeys screeching, and the deer jumping around. There was a tiger in sight. A group of men saw the big, yellow cat with black stripes on its body, staring ferociously at Jamal. Out of nowhere, another giant cat leapt out in front of that tiger and roared so loudly that the ground trembled. The new tiger fought off the attacker, then prowled towards Jamal and glanced at him before disappearing into the dense forest.

People who witnessed the miracle believed that Hiran had returned as a bagowa bhoot to save his son. It is still believed that Hiran wanders around the village to ensure his wife and children are safe.

Characteristics of the bagowa bhoot

- Has the form of a tiger.
- Is the spirit of a human killed by a tiger.
- Found in the Sundarbans delta.

6

BARUL

Dear Proloy da,

Spring is here once again. I don't know if that still makes a difference to you. It hadn't mattered to me either so far. But today it does. You always said, 'If winter is here, can spring be far behind?' Do inform your favourite poet that he was wrong. Winter lasted four years this time. Nowadays, in the afternoons, I can hear the windows squeaking in the spring wind. Although the squeaking keeps me awake even after I had taken my post-lunch medicine, I don't mind it. I want to take in every bit of this house before I have to leave.

In the past few years, I haven't participated in any cultural programmes—be it Rabindra Jayanti or the Durga Puja annual festivities. Does that surprise you or make you happy? I know you despised it when your friends commented that I looked gorgeous while dancing on the

stage. I always looked forward to spending afternoons in the attic when you'd playfully pull my hair and ask me strange questions like how dare I look pretty. I miss the kisses that ended those petulant fights.

But after a while, you stopped fighting with me. It was so strange seeing you smile like an idiot from your hospital bed. Do you remember how you would get annoyed at the doctor who teased me for sitting beside your bed all day and holding your hand even when you were unconscious? You hated seeing anybody showing any interest in me. I was annoyed at your extreme possessiveness; but deep down you knew that I liked the creative ways you came up with to deal with the neighbourhood boys who wrote me love letters. You had replied to all of them pretending to be me. One of them still thinks I practise black magic and runs away from his rooftop every time I go up to ours. I want to laugh at him, but I end up tearing apart inside. How do you feel now that I am going to belong to another man?

I had no choice but to agree to this marriage. I can imagine your eyes rolling with irritation, but my parents deserved a break from the stress of dealing with a psychotic daughter. Of course, I could go back to studies and live on my own, but that would make them unhappy. My psychiatrist was convinced that the only cure for me was to stay far away from my memories. Marrying an NRI seemed like the best option to my father. I still think of that day when he held my hand, begging me to lead a normal life. I still remember the stormy afternoon when my windows shattered and messed up my emotional state. I told you about it, didn't I?

I looked for you everywhere. Beginning from the primary-school backyard, to the mango tree where we first kissed. I am aware my father let me run wanton in my futile efforts. He was deeply agitated when I revealed my intentions to tell my future husband about my troubled past. I didn't want to be a burden in anyone's life. When I first met Mr Roy in the old garden and told him about you, about us, he kept watching the sparrow couple building a nest on the nearest tree. When I paused, trying to recover from the impact of saying your name out aloud for the first time in four years, he quipped that birds make one of the most inspiring couples in the world because each roam freely in the sky all day long, going anywhere they want, knowing they will end up in the same nest at the end of the day. He said he wanted a nest, even if that meant that he were the leaves circling my feet that evening in the rough wind. On my way back, I wasn't sure whether I was happy or sad, once I realized that with him, I wouldn't need to replace your memories. I didn't know why storms always show up on such significant days of my life.

But I understand now. Everyone says I'll be rid of my past as soon as I perform the marriage rituals. But I didn't listen to their warnings about the storm last evening and went to the rooftop. They will never see the eddies of wind that swirled around me, exactly seven times. I know it was you, Proloy da. I touched you before you melted into air.

As the flute sound announces my marriage in the month of March, I realize I can never let you go.

Until we meet again,

Mohor

Mohor went up to the terrace. Any moment, someone would call her to start getting dressed in her bridal attire. After reading the letter one more time, she tore it into pieces and scattered the shreds of paper from the edge of the terrace. Lifting the ends of her sari, she slowly climbed on the cornice. She felt the wind sweep her again, whirling the pieces of the letter around her. The wind forced her to step down from the cornice. Through tear-stained eyes, she watched every piece of her letter to Proloy da disappearing into the horizon.

Characteristics of the barul

- Forms an eddy of wind and swirls around.
- Usually appears during kalboisakhi, the evening storm.
- Sometimes appears out of nowhere and forms a whirl of wind.
- Completely harmless.
- Free spirit.
- Found in West Bengal.

7

BAYANGI

Some spirits can be tamed to become slaves for humans. The bayangi is a ghost that works in exchange for money. They are often summoned by black magic practitioners of the Konkan region for nefarious purposes.

The bayangi can be captured inside a coconut shell on a new moon day. Interested buyers can buy a coconut with a bayangi inside from a black magic practitioner.

The buyer then has to place the coconut in a remote corner of his house where nobody else would notice it. The occultist would instruct him on the offerings to be made to the ghost and how to set it free after a period of seven years.

The bayangi, despite being trapped, would bring vast amounts of wealth to its owner, and render everybody in his neighbourhood poor. Basically, the black magic vacuums wealth from the neighbours and gathers them into the home of the bayangi's owner.

But every time people force a free spirit into serving them, the spirit claims a much bigger price which cannot be paid for with money.

The flipside of availing the bayangi's services is that people get addicted to wealth easily. Nobody frees the bayangi even after the period of seven years is over. Soon after, the bayangi becomes restless and begins to show signs of anger.

Though the wealth accumulated due to the bayangi remains intact, gradually, those close to the owner start dying one by one— the nearest and the dearest ones catch deadly diseases and the loved ones start to move away.

There are many instances wherein brothers and sisters in joint families grew apart, or their offspring went insane or where spouses committed suicide—inevitably the tragic events took place after the person became successful. In all such cases, the people are suspected to have summoned the bayangi and kept them trapped for over seven years.

Characteristics of the bayangi
- Initially, a helpful ghost.
- Associated with black magic.
- Brings prosperity to the owner in exchange of family tragedies if kept for longer than seven years.

8

BESHO BHOOT

Besho bhoots are said to dwell in the eastern part of India. They are ghosts that reside in bamboo groves. Though they are feared as notorious killers, they are also believed to be extremely mischievous. In Bengal, they are known as the besho bhoots, whereas the Assamese call them the doula.

Branches of bamboo are flexible and sprout around bushes. They swish in the wind; some lay tangled on the ground. One accidental step on a fallen branch and the besho bhoot springs straight up. So, the ghost enables this tangling and springing, which is where the besho bhoot comes to play.

There are several rumours and folklores spread across a vast region. The following is one of the many stories from the villages of Birbhum district, in Bengal.

There once lived a grumpy man in the village. He never mingled with other villagers, never took part in village events, never allowed children to play on his grounds, and never missed an opportunity to be mean to others. Not a single person in the entire village liked him and the children were terrified of him.

One evening, he needed some bamboo stems, but since he never paid anybody back, nobody agreed to sell them to him. So, he decided to stealthily chop some from a neighbour's bamboo grove in the dead of the night. As soon as he saw one perfectly sized bamboo falling on the ground, he went and stood over the stem to pick it up. Suddenly, the bamboo sprung up out of nowhere, injuring him.

The man was startled and started groaning in unbearable pain. Someone laughed and clapped through the bamboo bush, and he realized he had been the victim of the besho bhoot.

From that moment on, the man changed completely. He became the biggest contributor during social events and created a playground for all the village children! The villagers wondered what could have happened to transform such a petty man. One day, while making preparations for a function, the villagers were lining the stage with bamboo stems when the man started running away chanting the name of Ram….

The villagers were not aware of any disease whose symptoms included the fear of bamboos but they understood that the man had encountered a besho bhoot.

Characteristics of the besho bhoot
- Lives in bamboo groves.
- Very mischievous, can be fatal.
- Found in eastern India.

9

BRAHMADAITYA

Vikash and his friends were disappointed that they had to attend a college located in the rural hinterland. None of them had gained admission into any of the good colleges in the city. This obscure village, on its way to becoming a township, was clearly disappointing for them as it was starkly different from what they had envisioned.

The infrastructure of the village had changed a lot in just a few years' time. Right after the construction of the college began, many people relocated to the village for work, and some started new businesses nearby. By the time the college was set up, new street markets had sprung up and the supply of goods from the big cities had become more regular. New medical centres were established, and pitch roads were built to make commutation easier. The villagers' simple daily lives were disrupted with all these new developments, but it was all for the better. Ponds were filled up, old buildings demolished, ancient trees cut down to make space for new construction and roads. The elders weren't happy about it, but the younger generation was excited about the future.

The students of the college lived in a local building that was located on the outskirts of the village, a ten-minute walk from the college. To introduce some urban culture, the students had turned the local club into a place to sit around and have some drinks and fun in the evenings. The elders of the village disapproved, but the boys, indifferent to their complaints, continued doing as they pleased.

The other place they spent time was under the old bael tree. The main road swerved around the tree. The boys would laugh at the foolishness of the road builders who could have saved a great deal of money and time by simply chopping down the tree and keeping the road straight. Hearing this, Pal Babu, one of the old men who'd always complain about the college boys' activities, was furious. 'How dare you boys drink under the holy tree? Do you know who lives here? Mukherjee babu. The brahmadaitya of this village.'

In response, the boys roared with laughter.

'That is great, grandpa! Mukherjee dadu is welcome to join us. We have a spare bottle of rum.' Vikash said in a drunken voice.

'For God's sake, don't you people respect the elders or the dead? Mukherjee babu was a very generous man. He founded this village and helped so many people acquire land. Unfortunately, he died too early, but he still keeps an eye on us. They couldn't cut this tree down even while constructing this useless road.'

'Oh, please! We'd love to meet this saviour and perhaps take a selfie with him.' Raucous laughter followed their remarks.

Pal Babu left the place fuming. He realized it was pointless to argue with these adamant fools. Vikash and his gang kept laughing at this ridiculous story all the way to their hostel. But one of the boys went pale. He quietly said he had heard the clip-clopping of wooden clogs but didn't see anybody. Another boy added that he saw someone with a white shawl walking around in wooden slippers late at night. Vikash, the leader of the group, was irritated at how easily his compatriots were shaken. He announced that he'd stay awake that night to find out what was going on. It wasn't a hard task; they had so much to laugh about that night that midnight passed. Vikash and two other boys crouched behind a low wall in a building backyard where the brahmadaitya had apparently been spotted.

And then, all at once, they saw him—a frail figure clomping along in wooden slippers. He was wearing a dhoti, and a white shawl was wrapped around his face and body. The slippers made a *clog-clog* sound as he moved. He walked close to the building, turned around, walked away, and then came back again, as though he were out for a stroll.

Vikash jumped up, followed by the other boys. Noticing that the figure had stopped, the boys ran towards him. The figure started running away, but his feet tripped over his dhoti and he fell. Laughing loudly, the boys pulled off the shawl to discover Sen Babu—one of the old men who had objected to their gang. This was a treat for the boys. Sen Babu tried to stand up, clearly embarrassed and anxious. But Vikash gleefully pushed him again. Sen Babu fell headlong. The boys started pulling at his dhoti. The more he struggled to save his honour, the more fun the boys had.

Clog-clog-clog-clog. A chill ran up their spines. A tall figure, with a white thread around his bare upper body, wearing a dhoti and wooden slippers boldly walked past. He looked like a fleeting shadow; a soft, white glow emanating from his body. Something about its presence made the boys feel faint. A strange, warm glow filled their hearts.

Three years later, the boys passed out from the college with distinction, and there has been no conflict since between the locals and the students of the college.

Characteristics of the brahmadaitya

- A beneficent spirit.
- Very powerful but usually uses its powers to help people.
- Should not be insulted.
- A watchful protector of the villages/houses.
- Always wears dhoti and wooden slippers with the paita (holy thread) on their bare chest.
- Sometimes has a tuft of hair on the back of the head.
- The ghost of unmarried Hindu Brahmin man with knowledge and respect at his living age.
- Mostly helps keep an eye on the locality he inhabits.
- Sometimes helps people or blesses them with boons.
- Can be seen on the branches of bael trees.

10

BRAHMARAKSHASA

The brahmarakshasa is considered one of the most powerful evil spirits in Hindu mythology. These evil spirits arise upon the death of any pestiferous Brahmin with a track record of misusing his knowledge of the scriptures. And so, their souls remain bound to the earth to pay for the sins they had committed in their lifetimes.

The brahmarakshasa has a disturbing appearance, usually found hanging upside down from trees. They have grotesque features and two fatal horns.

Equipped with the knowledge of the Vedas and Puranas, the brahmarakshasa can grant boons and bless others with material benefits. They are also cursed with the qualities of the rakshasa, or demons, as they eat humans. Only a handful of people can defeat the brahmarakshasa. If provoked, these creatures can also turn humans into piles of ashes.

In central and southern India, the brahmarakshasas are worshipped. In some places, builders make offerings to these spirits

before starting a construction. There is even a temple dedicated to them in Kerala.[*]

In countries such as Thailand and Cambodia which have been influenced by Hindu culture and Sanskrit literature, references to the brahmarakshasa can be found. There is the local culture of keeping a shrine beside households as a tribute to these spirits.[**]

In popular culture, a Yeti-like brahmarakshasa was most recently found rampaging in a 2014 horror Hindi film *Creature 3D*, but this depiction failed to refer to the mythological origins of the spirit.

Characteristics of the brahmarakshasa

- The spirit of a Brahmin who misused religious scriptures.
- Can bless human beings, but can also be fatal to them.
- Worshipped in parts of South–central Asia.

---

[*] The Thirunakkara Shiva temple in Kottayam has a separate temple dedicated to the brahmarakshasa.

[**] Sir Charles Eliot, *Hinduism and Buddhism: An Historical Sketch*, London: Routledge & Kegan Paul, 1921.

11

CHANDA

The chanda is a supernatural creature with a unique origin story. This ghost is not as 'natural' as the others; it does not arise upon someone's death; gods do not create it. It is created by humans.

Like the bayangi (see chapter 7), the chanda owes its existence to black magic practitioners in the eastern part of India, ranging from Bengal to Assam. The process of creating a chanda is grotesque. To begin with, a young Brahmin boy has to be murdered. Then, the gunins who practise spiritual rituals by using various small objects like flowers or human bones extract one bone from the dead body and perform certain black magic practices and generate a ghost called mayabi (illusional) chanda. Not all gunins are powerful enough to perform the process; only a few of the most skilful ones who are dedicated enough to their dark arts can perform the entire process without being interrupted by other surrounding spirits.

Chandas can enhance the power and influence of the gunins on the supernatural realm. If a gunin manages to create a chanda it will make him superior to the other gunins, as well as provide him

with control and knowledge about the actions and whereabouts of the ghosts around him.

The name chanda has been around for quite a long time. In the Puranas, the goddess Chamunda was named Chanda after she killed two asuras named Chanda and Munda.

Characteristics of the chanda

- Malevolent spirit created by gunins.
- Can be deadly in encounter.
- Found in eastern India.

12

CHEDIPE

In the Telugu language, the word chedipe literally means 'sex worker'. The chedipe is essentially a vampire who is at times portrayed as a sorceress or a witch, and at times as a naked lady riding a tiger underneath a moonlit sky, and at other times as a shapeshifter wandering around as a tiger with one human leg. Chedipe is thought to be a slave of the gods residing in Hindu temples.

The chedipe is adept in hypnotizing its victim, just like many other vampiric creatures. They target a household and use their hypnotic powers to put everyone under a trance so that people do not wake up to the sound of their actions once they have gained entry into the victim's house. One way in which the chedipe is thought to attack its victim is by biting the toes of the strongest man in the household and sucking the blood out of the man's body. Some chedipe portray themselves as the succubus who is believed to have sex with the strongest man in the house while everyone sleeps. No matter which way it chooses to attach itself, a chedipe

brings impurity to the family. The men would wake up weaker each passing day with no memory of what has happened to them at night, and the chedipe would return again and again, until the men gradually die.

They cannot invade a house where idols of gods are worshipped with incense sticks, mantras, and other religious rituals. When the chedipe attacks men in the forest in a tiger form, they flee if the man responds to its attack with a weapon in his hand. Also, if a person recognizes that the tiger is actually a chedipe (because it has one human leg), it will go back to its original form, hide, or pretend as though it is digging for medicinal roots in the forest.

Folklore suggests that chedipe are part of an undead species, or dangling between life and death. The souls of women who die of causes like suicide or during childbirth as well as those involved in sex work are believed to turn into a chedipe.

Characteristics of the chedipe
- Encounter with it can be fatal.
- Kills its victim by sucking the blood out of their bodies or having sex with them until their bodies can take it no longer.

13

CHETKIN

Ramesh went to the toilet breathing heavily. He felt better after splashing cold water on his face. It took him a while to look at the mirror. Mustering up his courage, he looked up at his reflection and then around the toilet in the mirror. There was nothing there but he double-checked anyway. His heart was still racing from the memory of his narrow escape from death moments ago.

He tried to go to sleep but it was difficult. Perhaps it was time he sought help. Initially he thought the motionless eyes staring back at him from the rear-view mirror of his car had been a hallucination. He even thought he smelled a foul odour which had been coming from something inside the car. But today, when he found that dog sitting right in front of his car, he got an uneasy feeling again that it was giving him the same blank stare that had been haunting him for months. Ramesh closed his side mirror and turned the rear-view mirror away to stop himself from looking at the eyes. Back on the highway, he could smell that foul odour again and he realized this smell only came when he spotted the frozen stare of the eyes in his rear-view mirror. He couldn't stop himself from fixing his mirror to look at the back seat. The petrifying, cold eyes looked back at him. He lost his focus and almost hit the road divider. His reflexes kicked in, and he narrowly averted an accident. But the trauma of that moment still gave him the shivers, and he couldn't sleep that night.

Next morning Ramesh decided to speak to Prakash, his closest friend at work. The trouble had started nearly a year ago with an accident. After avoiding the topic for almost a year, maybe they needed to talk about the incident again. The vision of the couple with their child lying still on the highway on the outskirts of Mumbai flashed before his eyes. Prakash had been driving the car that night, since Ramesh was drunk. They slowed down as they passed the spot where the family's motorbike had been smashed, maybe hit by a truck. The blood-stained road had made Ramesh sick and they drove away. What had haunted them for months was that the child had still been alive. They could have saved him. Instead, they saved themselves from the night's trouble and taking on any responsibility of an orphan.

Prakash knew that guilt was still haunting his friend. They had escaped, but the night was fast closing on them. Perhaps they should stop running and face it head on. He proposed that they return to the site of the accident but Ramesh, who was a lot more traumatized than Prakash realized, was reluctant. Prakash grew more determined in the face of his friend's reluctance.

It all started one afternoon after a few days. Ramesh could smell the foul odour each time he got in the car. Nonetheless, he had accepted Prakash's suggestion. Since Ramesh was unwilling, Prakash agreed to drive. They kept their eyes fixed on the road.

Both of them had avoided this road for a year. Still, it wasn't difficult to find the exact spot of the accident. As it was on the other side of the highway, they took a U-turn at the next exit and slowed down in front of a signboard that read, 'Mumbai 10 km'.

It took them a while to get out of the car. Naturally there was no sign of the accident. None of them could speak a word. After standing there for a few minutes, they got into the car again. They didn't know whether they felt better or worse. They just kept driving lazily. Dusk slowly rolled over the horizon. The road seemed unending, and both of them wanted to be home as early as possible. Prakash checked the next signboard to estimate their arrival time. It read 'Mumbai 10 km'. He stopped the car with a jerk.

'Hey, what's wrong? Why did we stop?' Ramesh asked.

'It's her, the mother. She is at the spot.'

Ramesh laughed.

'I thought I was the one having hallucinations. What's wrong with you? Let's keep moving.'

Prakash tried to calm down but his heart was beating wildly. In the last remaining light of the day, the woman stood there looking straight at him. Her spine-chilling, motionless stare penetrated his heart. He didn't want to bother Ramesh any more and started the car again. Driving past the terrifying figure, he desperately looked for the next milestone. This time he could identify the area even before reading the signage. It was completely dark by then, and Prakash tried not to look too hard for the woman this time. He put his foot down on the accelerator and shot past the spot.

'We need to find a way out; maybe we should drive on the wrong side for a while on the other side of the road. What do you think, Ramesh?'

Ramesh didn't answer. Prakash suddenly felt a vile stench fill the car. He looked at his friend, whose motionless eyes were fixed on him. Prakash lost his focus at high speed. He saw the sign with 'Mumbai 10 km' one last time before he hit the brake hard—the car bucked violently and flipped over to the side of the road.

Characteristics of the chetkin

- Kills people by causing accidents, usually road accidents.
- Has a foul smell.
- If a woman dies in a road accident, she turns into this spirit.
- Found in parts of Maharashtra.

14

CHIRBATTI

Never before did a road look like such a dead end to Prateek. He knew it was going to be a bad day when he missed the first bus and had to take the next one. It was already late afternoon when he got off at the small town from where he had to take a local cart so that he could reach the village located in the middle of nowhere. As he had scored average marks in his selection exam, he wasn't posted to any of the main cities and had to opt for this interior village near the Rann of Kutch. The prospect of a government job is impossibly tempting. Prateek hoped that perhaps after a few years of dedicated service in this isolated outpost, he would be transferred to a decent city.

His optimism notwithstanding, he was discouraged by the fact that he hadn't managed to get on the right bus. When the bus he was on dropped him off, it was about to go dark. He hailed a cart and they trailed off. Pratik knew he'd have to walk a mile after the cart dropped him off at a point on a road close to the village, but he couldn't possibly imagine what it was like until the cart driver pointed at nothing but the darkness ahead of him. When the last glow of light coming from the cart faded away, Prateek looked hopelessly at the road and blamed his whole life and the events that led him to his gloomy fate. He could only see some hundred metres of the road ahead of him. Beyond that, pitch-black darkness.

As long as there is a track, it must lead to somewhere. He pulled himself together and started walking. It was harder than he thought. After walking for almost half an hour he couldn't understand if he was still on a road or just walking through the ridges of the lands separating one plot from another. He thought maybe he should go back and wait on the main road for a cart back to the township and return in the morning. He turned back, but the path leading back was just as dark as the one ahead. As far as his eyes could see, there was not a single glimmer of light from a car or a house.

Hopelessness pulled him down. A heavy feeling in his bones rooted him to the spot. The starry night above his head looked darker than he was used to, but that also meant that the stars were brighter. He took one last glance at the endless darkness and started walking randomly about.

Then he saw it: two small globes of lights piercing the darkness at a distance. The more he looked towards the lights the brighter they started glowing. They were like small fires inside a lantern.

He felt a ray of hope inside him. It must be some of the villagers out in the fields. He must be close to his destination or could at least ask for directions. He started walking hastily towards the lights, keeping his eye fixed on them.

They weren't really still. One of the lights kept moving, and the other followed it. The two lights would collide with each other and fall to ground. Then, when the first one got up from the ground and moved away swiftly, the other did the same. Confused, Prateek stopped for a second. These had to be kids playing with each other. They must have escaped from the elders and wandered off to play in the night. He grew hopeful because this meant the village was closer than he thought.

The lights continued playing with each other. Running away from each other, then coming closer and colliding again, only to fall on the ground and roll over one another. One floated a little bit higher off the ground than normal. Did someone just throw the lantern in the air? This must be a dangerous game, yet they seemed very comfortable moving about with each other.

Something was odd. Prateek was no longer on the road or even the ridges; a thick swamp was beginning to suck at his feet. He felt like he had been walking for a long while, but the lights remained exactly where they were. He didn't know what else he could do; it was somehow impossible to take his eyes off the lights. He felt as if nothing existed any more, as if the whole dark land and the starry canopy was the canvas for their enigmatic game. By then Prateek knew they weren't playing. They were making love. Towards the horizon they floated mingling and caressing each other. He knew he had to follow them—nothing had ever seemed so obvious. Up in the air they floated, wrapped tightly in each other's embrace. Fading slowly into the starry horizon, as if they were two shooting stars, only this time they didn't fall from the sky, rather launched towards it and couldn't be identified any longer in the crowd of stars massing overhead.

Prateek fell to his knees. He felt like he had just woken up from a dream. Startled, he looked around. It was unmistakably the outskirt of a village. He could see the walls of a small primary school, the soft glow rising from lanterns in huts nearby.

He heard about the couple next morning. The lovers who couldn't fulfil their love during their lifetime because they belonged to different religions. They ended their life on the fields one night. But the couple could still be seen making love in the fields on some nights. Nobody could stop the lovers from being with each other any longer.

Characteristics of the chirbatti

- People who lost their ways in the swamps or the fishermen who died at work become the chirbatti.
- Mostly harmless.
- Appear as floating lights over water bodies or swamps. Those who follow these lights might lose their minds or even get lost forever.
- Sometimes help lost travellers to their destinations.

15

CHIROGUNI

My research into supernatural beings threw up an interesting fact—that the majority of ghosts were originally female. This is due to the fact that women have been oppressed, tormented, and even bullied since the beginning of recorded time by men, their families, as well as patriarchal societies. Most women could not express their sorrow and grief during their lifetimes, and thus folklore suggests that these ghostly manifestations are ways in which they have finally been able to express themselves

In Bengali folklore, the souls of the women who die during childbirth are said to be trapped in the mortal world as an evil ghost spirit known as the chiroguni. They are depicted as wandering spirits who lurk in deserted spaces, crematoriums, and around waterbodies. They wander in search of humans so that they can possess their bodies and minds. When someone is possessed by a chiroguni, along with behavioural changes, their body temperature also begins rising and they begin uttering gibberish.

If children are possessed by the chiroguni they start dancing in a

frenzied manner and sing at the top of their lungs. Folklore suggests that this behaviour derives from the chiroguni's unfulfilled wish to love children, as in their lifetimes they breathed their last breaths before their children could open their eyes. This sort of haunting is typical of the ghosts of women who die during childbirth. In other manifestations, the chiroguni tries to stop people from leading fulfilling lives and tries to lead them to an early death, spoiling their chance at parental affection. Villages are known to summon an occultist or a black magic practitioner to save those possessed by the chiroguni.

Characteristics of the chiroguni

- A female spirit, usually malevolent.
- Possesses both children and adults.
- Thought to be ghosts of women who died during childbirth or were oppressed.
- Found in many villages in India.

16

CHORDEWA

Priya wanted a boy. She knew nobody in her highly educated family would disrespect her for looking forward to having a boy, as it was her personal preference. When she eventually gave birth to a little boy who brightened their sixteenth-floor apartment, she was ecstatic. On the other hand, her husband, Mukesh, was just happy that both the mother and child were healthy.

Priya's mother had been in bed for months with a slipped disc, and so was unable to come over and take care of her daughter. So, her mother-in-law agreed to stay with them. Since most of the chores were done by the midwife, Priya wondered why her mother-in-law had turned up so suddenly. The mother-in-law forbade her from going out of her room and made Priya do all her chores herself. Having grown up in a modern, educated family, Priya could not handle the restrictions that were being imposed upon her. She expected her husband to step in and bend some rules, but Mukesh, an obedient son, stayed quiet. He, too, couldn't enter her room since it was considered impure (usually twelve

days after childbirth). He and his mother would come to talk to Priya from the door. Of all the things she had to put up with, her husband's indifference agonized her the most.

She'd sometimes talk to Nidha, the kind and helpful midwife, to get over her boredom. Whenever she felt like a prisoner, Nidha provided the only touch of kindness she experienced in the whole of the day. While her husband and mother-in-law were asleep, she would take care of the baby and let Priya take a walk. But Priya was deeply upset at her husband's behaviour. Nidha would stay with her till late evening and sometimes help Mukesh and his mother with dinner. Priya would sometimes watch all three of them sitting at the dinner table laughing at a joke Mukesh had cracked. She missed his sense of humour and felt even more annoyed with his mother.

As the days passed, Priya started watching Mukesh, Nidha, and her mother-in-law enjoying themselves. Nidha started spending more time with the others rather than looking after her or the baby. Priya couldn't suppress a pang of jealousy when she saw her huddled up with Mukesh one day. Every evening, when her mother-in-law was busy with the TV, both of them would sit in the hall to chat. Annoyed, Priya started making excuses to call Nidha to her room to do various chores. Soon after this, Mukesh came to her door one day and confronted her for being abusive towards the poor midwife. Shocked and heartbroken, Priya tried to seek her mother-in-law's help, but to no avail.

Priya, sensing what was going on, decided to catch Nidha and Mukesh red-handed. One night after dinner when all the rooms went dark, she quietly opened the door to her room and tiptoed across to the room that Mukesh and her had shared before the baby arrived. She had a good idea of what she would find. When she caught them, she would get rid of that woman and then deal with her husband.

She opened the door of the bedroom. In the dimly-lit room, Mukesh was sleeping peacefully. Priya felt ashamed; she couldn't bear to admit all the foul things she had imagined about them. Feeling lighter, she walked back to her room. She opened the door and was shocked to see Nidha standing inside. She called her by her name and Nidha turned around. She had the baby hanging upside down by his feet, with her serpent-like tongue wrapped around the little head. She stared at Priya with her dilated black eyes and the door closed behind her with a click.

Characteristics of the chordewa

- Malevolent ghost that preys on mothers and newborn babies.
- Often kills the mother and child.
- Takes the form of a woman.
- Found in Maharashtra.

17

CHUDAIL

The chudail or churel is a female paranormal creature which is to be encountered in myths, tales, folklore, grandmother's tales, and eyewitness accounts all across South and Southeast Asia, especially in the Indian subcontinent. The word is also a local slang for witches in the Hindi language. They are the ghosts of women who have died due to extreme suffering like childbirth, difficult pregnancies or, sometimes, due to the torture inflicted by the in-laws.

Capable of taking animal shapes, the chudails are described as grotesque-looking in their true forms. They are known by different names in different regions, 'Petni' or 'shankchunni' in Bengal, and 'pontianak' in Malaysia and Indonesia.

Although they are identifiably female in form, their bodies are misshapen and grotesque with saggy breasts, black tongue, thick, rough lips and sometimes, without any face at all. Sometimes the chudail is dressed in white clothes, sometimes she roams around naked with her feet facing backwards.

The concept of chudails as the ghosts of ill-fated women can be traced back to Persia, where they were believed to be the spirits of women who died during their 'period of impurity'. In Southeast Asia, this period is described as the time between pregnancy and childbirth and in India, and it also comprises of menstrual cycles and the first twelve days after childbirth.

Other sources tell a different story about the origin of the chudail. They could be the undead spirits of the baby girls who died within twenty days of being born. Or, they could rise from women who died as virgins, or before they were married, or had unsatisfied desires.

The chudail hunts down the men of the family that had caused her suffering. The youngest man would be targeted first, followed by the rest, one by one. They can also infect people with deadly diseases and snatch the souls of anybody who responds at night to someone unknown calling out their names. After killing the men of the family, the chudail go after teenage boys, make love to them, and seduce them to meet her in the afterlife.

In Hindu mythology, chudails are believed to become witches or dakinis who serve Goddess Kali to defeat any evil forces. An unsatisfied soul or chudail can be appeased by sacrificing a goat and performing certain religious rituals. There are other methods to prevent the creation of chudails. Some preventive measures include, but are not limited to, taking good care of a pregnant woman, and if she dies, a strict funeral should be conducted according to rituals to satisfy her soul.

Characteristics of the chudail

- A female spirit.
- Very deadly, encounters are usually fatal.
- Usually kills men.
- Found all over South Asia and Southeast Asia.

18

DAAG

Mohan threw the piece of paper at the old man's face in disgust. Feeling helpless, he wondered what he could do to establish order on this estate. He had not imagined these old, uneducated farmers to be so fearless. The harvest they brought to Mohan, who was the estate manager, always weighed less than what he expected. Sceptical, Mohan decided to weigh the crop at the fields with his guards standing there, and then weigh them again at the storehouse. Just as he expected, the quantities did not tally.

Mohan knew the job of an estate manager was tough. He had to be harsh to maintain discipline. He had been advised to use the whip if necessary. So far, he hadn't used it, but maybe it was time. Annoyed, he went to the estate bungalow to his wife and two sons, who didn't dare say a word to him all day. By evening, he had decided to visit one of the fields as they were loading the crops on to the trailer of the tractor.

Throughout the loading process, he kept a close eye on the weighing machine and filled up the form himself. Satisfied, he started for the storeroom along with the tractor.

'Please leave the crops on the ground, sir.'

A thin old man was blocking his way. Mohan recognized him as one of the farmers who had been punished a couple of months ago. His monthly wages were stopped for a few months and the whole family had starved for days before Mohan had relented. How dare he openly challenge the estate manager?

'And why should I do that?'

'Please, sir. It will destroy all of us. You have to leave some of the yield for the daag.'

'That ghost again? Trust me, the estate is scarier than a ghost story.'

'No, sir. Good luck.'

With that, he got out of the way. At the storehouse, the weight of crops matched the weight taken at the field and Mohan was satisfied. He continued this method for the rest of the month. Although it was exhausting for him to visit all the fields himself, the month-end results were so satisfactory it was worth all the stress. On the last day of the month, he returned home feeling happy; he had bought his favourite peras along with other delicacies for a sumptuous dinner. But at the dinner table, his wife said there were no peras among the groceries. Furious, Mohan went to the kitchen to see for himself—there were no peras!

The next morning, he started for a meeting with his employer with a box full of files and reports detailing how the estate was faring. But when he arrived, he realized that a chunk of files was missing from the set. When his car arrived at the warehousing area in the evening, he saw that one of the granaries had caught on fire.

'You should have given the daag its share, sir. Now, it will destroy you!' a warehouse worker said, weeping.

The warehouse workers tried their best to put out the fire, all to no avail. The granary was burnt down to the ground. Disconcertedly, Mohan made a record of the losses, and went home, where worse news awaited him. One of his sons was missing.

His wife wept as she told him this. Mohan knew there was no point in searching for him. He started straight for the village. Maybe he should have visited these homes earlier rather than only going to the fields. The huts looked so wretched; he realized these people were really poor. Maybe they had always been as helpless as he felt right now.

He called a meeting with everyone and announced that he will be allocating crop from one of the fields as a tribute to the daag. Whatever was harvested there need not be transported to the storehouse. He summoned a few elders and walked towards that field. It was almost dusk, and he saw a silhouette of a body lying there. His missing son was sleeping in the field.

Characteristics of the daag
- A type of field demon.
- Demands a portion of crops after harvest.
- Only harms people who refuse their share from the crops.
- Found in Uttar Pradesh.

19

DAKAN SAKAN

She pulled the rope again. The unyielding silence of the night was broken by the sound of the pulley. The well felt like a bottomless abyss and she didn't know for how long she had been trying to get the bucket out. The bucket was stuck; she tugged harder. This time it came out smoothly. She upturned the bucket over her head and thick smoke came out of it. The smoke engulfed her shoulders first, then her chest. It took a while for it to cover her pregnant belly.

Jyoti woke up with a jerk. She was sweating all over. There was a sharp pain in her head, and she clutched her pregnant belly. It was such a horrible dream. She must have screamed, since her husband, Veer, woke up as well. Used to his wife's erratic behaviour, he calmly brought her a glass of water.

'What was it this time?'

'Just a bad dream.'

'You have to face it, Jyoti. The doctor said you need to look into the eyes of your "invisible observers" to get rid of them forever. How is the headache?'

Jyoti knew her husband was worried about her. This was her fourth pregnancy and he was trying his best to support her. It was a very difficult case for their gynaecologist as well since there was technically nothing wrong with her other three pregnancies. When the doctors couldn't figure out what was causing her chronic headaches, they referred her to a psychologist. After many sessions of counselling, Jyoti confessed that she had a fear of being followed all the time. She saw shadows behind her in mirrors and felt like someone was watching her in empty rooms. The doctor concluded this was the result of the trauma of multiple miscarriages. He advised that if she felt she was being followed or watched, she should turn around and face her fears. This helped and Jyoti felt better; but she still had nightmares which bothered the doctor.

'Have you considered visiting your old home in Punjab like the doctor suggested?' Veer asked.

'No! I'm not ready for it.'

'Jyoti, you need to understand. We cannot take any chances this time.'

She panicked and promptly agreed to do as the doctor had suggested. She had left Punjab years ago for studies, before getting married and settling down in Mumbai. Her parents visited her in Mumbai a couple of times but she had not visited her home town again. When the doctor suggested that she face her fears, this was the first thought that entered Veer's mind. Perturbed with her indifference towards her roots, Veer was relieved that Jyoti agreed without much hesitation.

For somebody like Veer, born and raised in a big city, a village like the one Jyoti belonged to was a little overwhelming. He spent all his days wandering around the pond and strolling through the rice and cane fields. Jyoti accompanied him sometimes but otherwise kept to herself in her old room. She seemed cheerful and that made Veer optimistic.

One day as he was walking around the back of the house, he found an abandoned well with dirty water at the bottom. When he found out that Jyoti had met with an accident in the well as a child, he tried to talk to her about it, but she refused to reveal more.

One morning, he woke up to find Jyoti missing. After searching the house, he went outside and found her at the back of the house leaning on the parapet of the abandoned well and peering inside.

He convinced her to come inside and talk about it.

'You wanted me to face it, remember? It wants me to face it, too!'

'There is nothing inside the well Jyoti, only darkness.'

'Exactly! The darkness wants to come out.'

Veer didn't know how to bring her back to her senses. Feeling helpless, he discussed this with her parents and realized it was a bad idea that she visit the well. They got very anxious, asked him to lock Jyoti in the room that night and leave with her the next morning. Distressed, Veer kept his wife close that night, but she remained very silent. He didn't bother her that night and fell into an uncomfortable sleep.

The muffled sound of scraping metals interrupted his disturbed sleep. When he woke up, Jyoti was not in the room. Reflexively, he walked to the well. In the dark, Veer saw her pulling a bucket out of the well. Maybe she was right. Maybe it was darkness that she had pulled from the void. She held the bucket upside down above her head as if she were taking a bath. In the moonlight, Veer could see a pool of blood between her legs. There was no baby bump any more. She looked at him with a strange smile, 'It was a girl!'

Characteristics of the dakan sakan
- A shapeless ghost.
- Causes illness in the womb and the mind of a pregnant woman.
- Lives in residential areas.
- Kills people.
- Found in Punjab.

20

DAKINI

The dakini is considered a carnivorous, bloodthirsty avatar of Goddess Kali, who devoured asuras[*]. Her supernatural form makes an appearance in medieval legends. Although primarily a Hindu concept, the idea of the dakini permeated into Buddhism and further into Japanese culture and Tibetan Buddhism. Dakinis are full of energy and their movement releases energy into space.

Dakinis have been classified into different groups. According to Tibetan lamas, there are prajnaparamita, the dakini of mandala, outer dakini, and yogini. According to the trikaya doctrine, there are dharmakaya, sambhogakaya, and nirmanakaya dakinis[**].

They are associated with the anuttarayoga tantra, representing

---

[*]The term asura first appeared in the Vedas, and refers to a human or divine leader. Its plural form gradually predominated and came to designate a class of beings opposed to the Vedic gods. Later the asuras came to be understood as demons.

[**]Judith Simmer-Brown, *Dakini's Warm Breath: The Feminine Principle in Tibetan Buddhism*, Boston and London: Shambhala Publications, 2002, pp. 69–79.

the path of transformation, and convert negative emotional energy into positive luminous energy.

Characteristics of the dakini

- A supernatural avatar of Goddess Kali.
- Can be bloodthirsty and carnivorous but can also be benevolent.
- Encountered in myths and cultures of other countries including Japan and Tibet/China.

21

DAMORI

The damori is a supernatural entity believed to exist in a realm or space between mortals and spirits, somewhat similar to fairies and elves but different in every other aspect. They originate from an unseen and unnamed realm. In Tantric philosophy, especially in the region spread from Bengal to Assam, the damori are said to have no corporeal shape in their own realm but could take on a visible form when they appear in our world. Enthusiastic scholars of Tantra Sadhana would travel from their villages to the Kamrup–Kamakhya temples in Assam to learn black magic and worship evil supernatural entities using a method called bhoot damor. Unlike moha damor and kularnob, which invoke the gods and holy spirits, bhoot damor can be used to invoke controllable evil spirits and demi-goddesses like jogini or yogini, jokkjini, kinnori, apshori (which literally means fairies), bhutini, and such like. By chanting bhoot damor, they would eventually invoke a damori. The damori would be under the tantric's control for all kinds of nefarious purposes.

The practice of black magic and the Tantra Sadhana are widespread especially in the villages of East and Northeast India. Apart from tantrics, there are other black magic practitioners like aghoris, kapaliks, kabirajs. These practitioners can cause harm to their victims and kill them, if need be, through spirits like the damori. A common method of killing their targets is to perform the 'Baan Mara' ritual, which causes its victim to die of vomiting blood.

Characteristics of the damori

- A spirit that dwells in a world between that of human and spirit.
- An encounter with the damori is usually fatal.
- Can be summoned and deployed by tantrics and other practitioners of magic to kill designated victims.
- Found mainly in the villages of Bengal and Assam.

22

DAYANI

Luscious. Rinki repeated the word in her head. This new word intrigued her. She wanted to use this word to surprise boudidi. Ever since boudidi had come into the house of the Mittir family, life had become easier for Rinki. Being the daughter of the family, she had always been neglected. Boudidi was dark-skinned too. As the wife of the youngest son, she was the most efficient contributor of the farmhouse. So, no one could directly overrule her. Rinki grew close to her from day one. Boudidi found in Rinki a silent companion in the village. She made sure Rinki went to school, which her family had been unable to make happen ever since the death of her mother.

Rinki was studious. She'd never let boudidi down by getting poor grades. Ever since boudidi had got pregnant, Rinki would spend hours sitting beside her on the cool balcony and chattering about what she had learnt that day. It was a bit annoying at times since boudidi was exhausted on most days. Often, she would fall asleep in the middle of their conversation. Pregnancy must be a tough job, Rinki thought. She had seen how the most powerful cow of their shed had died giving birth to its slender, pretty-eyed, black calf. They named the calf Kalindi. The villagers didn't really like the calf. Every day it was taken out to graze, someone would complain about the calf's evil gaze. It became a family joke until one day, someone came shouting that their grandmother had died because she tried to feed Kalindi that day. Believing the calf to be ill-omened, they had beaten the calf with bamboo sticks and dumped her beside the river. The family tried to protest but didn't dare to go against the furious mob.

But Rinki couldn't let it go that easily. Thinking about the poor calf, she went looking for her the next day. Rinki could see the calf from a distance, lying in the dense shade of a banyan tree. She went up to it. The calf was still alive, drawing its last breaths. Rinki didn't know what kept it alive. She sat beside the shivering body, gently stroking its body. Suddenly, the calf stopped moving. Rinki felt a shiver running up her spine. This was the first time she had seen something die in front of her eyes. She stumbled home, was sick the entire week, and it took her months to get over the lifeless eyes of the calf that the villagers were so afraid of.

◆

Boudidi was busy. Rinki had just started having fun learning English, but boudidi, busy with her newborn son, couldn't find much time for her. Rinki tried to help her by keeping company with the baby. She didn't find babies particularly appealing, especially when they started howling for attention. She'd usually sit beside the baby while boudidi or somebody else took care of the kid. Their grandmother was very fond of the youngest son. Every morning she would take the kid out in the sun and rub oil on him. Sometimes Rinki would sit there with them. The small body didn't look that bad in the sun. The shiny oil glistened on the smooth dark skin making the baby look rather pleasing to the eyes. Now she understood why everybody loved to hold babies in their arms. The baby was like a dough of flour you needed to knead with your hands. Like a plump ball of flesh that would melt in your hand if you squeezed it. She kept looking at it, 'Luscious…luscious….' she whispered. 'What are you looking at?' the grandma shouted with a tone of fear in her voice.

'Stop looking at the baby like that! You loathe him, don't you?'

Rinki looked away in shock. For a moment, she forgot that her grandmother was present! But what was she shouting about? Grandmother carried the baby into the house. Rinki sat there furiously. Everyone in the house was too sensitive about the new baby. What was so special about the annoying, tiny human? Waves of anger washed through her as she left the house. She felt furious at the kid and everything around him.

She came back to the house to find everyone tense. Boudidi was crying at the top of her voice along with grandmother and other women of the family. The baby was sick. His whole body had started shrinking. His jaw muscles seemed to be locked in place, his mouth gaped wide, and his body was shrivelled up, as if the blood was being drained out of the body.

'It was her! I saw her looking at the kid this morning…she ate him up!' Grandmother pointed at Rinki and howled.

Rinki was frightened. She had witnessed this sort of scene before. She kept running until she reached the river. Frustrated and exhausted, she fell on her knees. Sobbing, she wondered why she felt so terrified. It wasn't the fear of getting beaten up. No, the terror running through her body and mind was coming from deep within her, wrapping up her spine, causing her stomach to churn. She wanted to expel the queasiness in her stomach. Jabbing a finger down her throat she belched, trying to take it all out. She tried again. This time, blood came out.

Characteristics of the dayani

- An evil power that captures living bodies. The possessed are believed to drink the blood out of anybody they look at.
- The dayani can jump from one body to another, and they do this frequently to stay alive. They can live for hundreds of years in this fashion.
- The only way to stop the dayani from migrating from one body to the next is by burning the body it possesses.
- Some are believed to be born with this evil in them.
- Extremely harmful. Can kill or cause severe physical damage to its prey.
- Many believe that the bodies start having their own magical abilities like witches.

23

DRAKSHI

Tribal tales are unique when it comes to describing unusual phenomenon. One such tale from the forests of western India talks about a demoness with daunting features. Belonging to the forest, the demoness resembles wild animals. Called the drakshi, it is covered in thick black fur and its huge muscular body haunts the deepest corners of the forest. Another bizarre detail is that it has green blood. The drakshi are believed to emerge from eggs lain by celestial demigods. In order to vanquish them, they must be doused with alcohol and set on fire.

A drakshi can be often mistaken for a wild animal. In *Chander Pahar* (1937), an adventure journey by Bibhutibhushan Bandopadhyay, the author describes a journey through a forest in Africa where the protagonist encounters a bunip who makes an enigmatic appearance. It has three very powerful fingernails and makes a coughing sound. It could still be considered an animal, but one key characteristic makes the drakshi (the bunip in the novel's African variant) deadlier than animals. If it bites someone, they also start having features similar to the drakshi. Slowly, they start acquiring features like thick fur all over the body, and green blood.

There exists a tale of the head-lady of a village who had acquired a lot of power by practising dark magic. She used to collect human skulls in her hut in order to perform witchcraft and captured anybody she wanted to. Hearing about this, the king of the most powerful village in the area captured the woman. Fearless, she claimed that she could control wild beasts. She was imprisoned and sentenced to a night inside a hut where free wolves would be her companions. Next morning, the beasts were mysteriously found dead. When the woman was released, everybody was so scared of her, that they kept their distance. Yet, the woman seemed more scared than anybody else and hardly left her own cottage. Gradually, people witnessed the transformation of the woman. It started with fur on her body. They thought her black magic must have gone wrong at some point, or taking control over wild creatures for days must have affected her physically. Once when she was weak, they attacked her in her hut. Green blood flowed. In her defence, she bit one of the other wives of her husband. But she was repentant and soon afterwards asked everybody to burn her along with her co-wife in alcohol to save their village.

Characteristics of the drakshi
- A malevolent demoness that is usually to be found forests of western India.
- Can pass on her dark traits to a victim by biting them.
- Is covered in thick fur, and has green blood.

24

DUND

There are stories of headless horsemen throughout the world. In many cultures, they are regarded as heroes—courageous fighters who lost their lives in great battles but are still around to protect us, even after losing their lives. They have several names in different parts of the country. In northern India they are known as dunds, and in Mirzapur they are known as baghesar, or tiger lord. Some myths say that the dunds are the undead spirits of the brave soldiers who fought in the war of Kurukshetra.

Dunds are glorious in appearance. They wear a soldier's armour, holding a big deadly sword in one hand and are always seen riding a horse. Dunds carry their heads with them, but the heads are not attached to their necks; instead, they are tied to either the handle of their swords or to their pommels.

The legends say that the dunds still wander around the places they once used to guard at midnight, ready to fight and protect those in their care should the need arise.

Characteristics of the dund

- Warrior demon riding a horse, a sword in one hand.
- Usually benevolent.
- Is usually headless.

25

EKANORE

In fairy tales and paintings, ghosts are often depicted with ears that look like winnows and teeth that look like radish. In Bengali folklore, we come across a ghost named ekanore who lives in palm trees and hunts naughty children. There are stories about mothers and grandmothers narrating tales about the ekanore in order to make restless children fall asleep quickly. The legendary music composer Salil Chowdhury has described the ekanore in a poem. He starts his poem with a rhyme he had heard from his grandmother.

Ekanore, Kanekore
Tentul pare, chhore chhore
Ek haathe taar nuner vanr, Arek haate chhuri
Kaan kete nun ghose beray bari bari.

Ekanore, with one ear
plucks bunches of tamarind!
With a pot of salt in one hand and a knife in the other,
he goes door to door, collecting ears and rubbing salt on them.

In Bengal, if someone has an ear lopped off, it is said that the individual has been punished for being shameless. And having 'du kaan kata', or lacking both of ears, is considered a sign of the absolute peak of shamelessness.

Ekanore is believed to have a huge collection of ears of the shameless. He is celebrated in a few well-known poems and folk tales.

Characteristics of the ekanore
- Usually a benevolent spirit.
- Is keen on punishing the shameless by lopping off one ear.
- Punishes naughty children.
- Has just one ear and one leg.

26

EKTHENGO

This story comes from a village where all the villagers had a unique habit. Every time they passed a bamboo grove that was located at the edge of the village, they hopped on one leg until the grove was at a safe distance behind them. They said it all started with the story of a boy many years ago.

Biltu and his friends used to idly spend their afternoons in the field that was on the other side of the grove. They didn't bother playing traditional games, but rather invented some of their own. One that was popular among them consisted of stacking bricks and jumping over them. Whoever was able to jump over the highest pile would win the game. Biltu always won this game.

The game took its own toll on the players. Once, Biltu's biggest rival, Pratik, made a desperate attempt to beat him and tripped over. Their gang laughed their heart out that day. Biltu couldn't hide the smile on his face each time he thought about Pratik tripping over the stack and pathetically rolling around on the ground. Pratik broke his leg and did not show up again.

Then, one day, a little while later, as the boys were picking up the best bricks safely in a corner of the field, they heard the sound of a stick. Pratik had turned up. Leaning on a stick he walked towards them, smiling broadly. While some of the boys admired his courage and welcomed him, Biltu and his close buddies weren't too happy.

'Why are you here, cripple? Still planning on another jump?' Biltu taunted.

'There's no need to be mean, Biltu. I knew you placed the broken brick on the stack that day; I didn't come after you, did I?' Pratik replied.

'How could you! Are you planning to chase me with a one-legged hop?'

Everyone cracked up at Biltu's rude sense of humour. Pratik went red in the face. The more he protested, the more fun the gang poked at him. They asked him to show how he hopped. On the verge of tears, he tried to leave. But Biltu wouldn't let it go easily. He snatched Pratik's stick and broke it into pieces. Falling over, Pratik managed to somehow stand on his good leg. He kept hopping to the end of the field, falling over many times, since he couldn't keep his balance, and then disappeared. The gang laughed till it was almost dark; they had just had one of the best afternoons ever!

Biltu was the last to set off for home. He smiled the entire way back. He was slightly worried as well since it was almost dark, and the adults might notice that it was long after he was expected to be home. He increased his pace while crossing the bamboo grove. The dry leaves on the ground made a rustling sound.

He could hear something else as well. A thudding sound was

following him, as though something heavy was falling on the leaves. He stopped. Two more thuds, and then the sounds stopped, too. Biltu looked around, but there was nothing to see. Just as he started walking again, he heard the sound again. He had an uneasy feeling that someone was following him. He tiptoed along, trying to make as little noise as possible. But the thuds grew louder. It was as if the noise was following him, and that someone was hopping behind him.

Biltu turned around with a shock. He saw a blurry dark figure at a distance, standing on one leg. He was quite sure it was Pratik.

'What are you doing here? Do you still have the courage to follow me? Haven't you tripped enough already?' Only, he couldn't laugh this time.

The figure didn't move. Neither did it show any signs of losing balance. Biltu didn't dare take his eyes off the figure. He took a step back to assess it. Then a few steps more. The figure made a steady hop towards him. Then another, and another. Something inside Biltu's head told him he should start running. He broke into the fastest run of his life. Unable to see where he was going, he tripped over a bamboo shoot and fell over. He realized he was bleeding from the knees when he tried to stand. But, his ankle had gone numb, and it gave way. With tears in his eyes, he looked back. There was nothing there. He tried to walk, but fell again. He wanted to leave that place as soon as possible. He started hopping on his good leg.

Ever since that day, every time someone would try to walk past the bamboo grove, they would come home with a fractured leg, babbling incoherently about the one-legged figure who had followed them, only to let them go when they started hopping along.

Characteristics of the ekthengo

- One-legged ghost.
- Folk tales about the ekthengo never really describe the rest of its body but it is believed to be like any normal human body.
- Sometimes this ghost is to be found alone; at other times it is part of a pack.
- Not very harmful. They just chase and scare people.
- Often found by a clump of bushes or grove of trees.

27

GALASI

Ravi always knew Sayan da could be a little harsh, but that night he had gone further than he could've imagined. It was obvious that the new boy, Hari, was a little foolish. From the days of his first year, Ravi knew that it was dangerous to be too smart or too stupid. Both attributes attracted attention of the seniors and they never left you until you were rid of your foolishness or smarts. They believed this was a necessary exercise that helped students blend in. Most students eventually ended up being good friends with the seniors even after leaving the hostel.

But staying alone could be really hard in the beginning for students like Hari. He came from a faraway village. Seemingly a first-generation learner, he was proud of his grades and top rank in the entrance examination. So much so that he forgot everyone in this hostel had excellent grades too. He wasn't special, and everyone took turns to remind him of that, coupled with some extra courses on how to get out of his comfort zone. Hari would begin arguments with his tormentors in his husky voice, which always made things worse. He could not understand how writing an essay on a porn video and sending it to a senior girl would help him with his career. He seemed particularly shy about girls, and this was the weakness the seniors had been waiting for. Sayan da took charge of tormenting Hari and forced him to hop around the backyard of the girls' hostel in his underwear. Everyone was entertained by the sight and soon fell to discussing the worst and most innovating cases of ragging they had seen or participated in. Hari returned to his room silently and sat on his bed. Sayan da, in-charge of the hostel wing, ordered everyone to leave him alone for the night so that Hari could calm down.

Ravi felt terrible for Hari. He, too, belonged to a small village and it gave him chills to simply imagine what he would have done if he were subjected to the same ridicule. After dinner, he went looking for Hari, who was still sitting on his bed. Ravi didn't know what to say. His other two roommates were keeping to themselves as well. Just when Ravi was about to leave the room, Hari smiled blankly.

Ravi's room was right next to Sayan da's. He could hear Sayan da and his three roommates still laughing about the events of the evening. They invited Ravi to join in, but he refused. Unable to sleep, he kept thinking about Hari's vacant smile. He probably should have said something, he thought. He went looking for him again.

Hari's bed was empty. The whole wing was quiet, which was slightly unusual since people usually stayed up almost until morning. Worried, Ravi kept looking everywhere. He even went downstairs in case Hari had gone looking for food.

He found Hari in the basement, searching for something in a pile of goods stacked in a corner. Ravi called him by his name, but he didn't seem to hear him. He ran towards Hari and turned him around. Hari looked at him with the same blank, expressionless eyes. Ravi tried to pull him away from the place but couldn't move him an inch.

Ravi didn't know what else he could do. On his way back, he called Sayan da, who said he was speaking to Hari right now. He was in their room telling them how he had grown up as an orphan in his uncle's house, and how the uncle used to beat him when things didn't go right. This college was his only way out of that hell, so he worked day and night to get a good rank and scholarship. Ravi could feel that Sayan da was trying to sound cool, but he that he was uneasy, too.

How had Hari managed to get upstairs so quickly? Nobody had passed him on his way up and there was no other way upstairs! Ravi felt uncomfortable and went back to the basement. His knees gave way the moment he walked in. Hari's lifeless body was hanging from the ceiling. His blank, expressionless eyes were still open.

When Ravi reached upstairs, he saw that the light in Sayan da's room was on. A husky voice, clearly audible in the silence of the night, was recounting a childhood story. Impatiently, Ravi pushed the door open. All four boys who shared the room were hanging by cable cords from the ceiling.

Characteristics of the galasi

- Makes people commit suicide by hanging themselves.
- When someone commits suicide by hanging, they can become this ghost.
- Kills people for revenge.
- Can be seen around a place where suicide has been committed.
- A ghost from Bengal.

28

GANDHARVA

A gandharva is a type of supernatural or celestial creature found in Hindu mythology. They are one among the eight celestial beings in Hinduism: asura, deva, garuda, kinnara, gandharva, mahoraga, naga, and yaksha.

They are the male counterparts of apsaras. Both gandharvas and apsaras are entertainers in the heavenly realm. The gandharvas sing Indian classical music with their peerless musical talent and the apsaras dance to that music.

Both celestial beings are examples of great beauty. Gandharvas are considered to be the most beautiful form of male beauty, and they are known to seduce women with their appearance and musical talent. Sexual encounters with gandharvas are said to cause insanity in women, but, with their divine powers, the gandharvas are said to heal people and restore virility. Apart from entertaining the gods, their other responsibility is to guard the soma rasa, a kind of intoxicant consumed by gods, and the elixir of immortality.

In Buddhism, these creatures are associated with the beauty

of trees and flowers. Gandharvas are mischievous and are known to disturb the meditation of monks. The Buddhist text, *Mahatanhasankhaya Sutta* mentions that for a baby to be planted in a mother's womb, three conditions must be met: first, the woman must be at the right stage in her menstrual cycle; second, she must have intercourse with a man; and third, a gandharva must be present at the scene. Other scholars have inferred that this could result in the gandharva becoming the child who is being born, as a result of its own karma.

In Jainism, gandharvas feature as celestial beings, devas. They are described as having golden-coloured skin by the Digambara sect, while the Svetambara sect depicts them with a dark complexion.

Gandharvas are considered one of the messengers who carry out conversations between heaven and earth. They are great warriors. When couples live together without being married their union is known as a gandharva marriage. The very famous masters of Indian classical music are also sometimes referred to as gandharvas.

Characteristics of the gandharva

- Celestial beings; the male equivalent of apsaras in Hindu myth.
- Sing beautifully; are also exquisite to look at.
- A beneficial and sometimes mischievous spirit.

29

GAYAL

A gayal is one of the very powerful ghost spirits in Indian folklore. Some sources say that gayals are the most powerful vampiric spirits ever recorded in the history of supernatural creatures. They are believed to possess the knowledge of what has happened in the past and what will take place in the future. They also have the ability to summon other ghost spirits to serve under their command, and sometimes, control their behaviour as well.

The gayal is born when a dead man is not provided with a proper religious funeral. The dead man's spirit rises from the grave and hunts down the people who should have buried him properly. It is believed that the concept of the gayal was created to ensure every man receives a proper burial after his death.

The primary purpose of the spirit is to take revenge from those who have wronged him. It will hunt down the person or the group of persons who should have provided him a proper burial. As is often the case, the first people to die for the sin of giving the spirit an improper burial are men from his own family, followed by men from his extended family. The gayal eats the flesh and drinks the blood of the people it attacks. After finishing the men from his own family, he would finish off other men that come in his way.

Gayals also attack pregnant women. They possess their body when they yawn or while they are eating. The spirit then takes away the life of both the unborn baby and the mother, consuming their energy from within.

There are rituals to keep the gayal inside the grave. If it does not find a human to kill, it mutilates other corpses in the burial ground. Consuming rotten flesh from other graves in the night, it stays inside its grave during the daytime.

So, to fool the gayal into believing it is daytime, people light candles and lights around the grave. Putting cups with holy water or Gangajal with raw milk beside the grave are ways to prevent the gayal from rising.

Young boys who wear a necklace with metallic elements like coins or the flower petals from certain gods such as Hanuman, Shiva, Durga, etc., in a metal encasing are said to be immune from attacks by gayals. Also, performing a proper burial of the dead man, or even completing the religious procedures which were left out in the first place makes the gayal less aggressive, if not completely benign.

Characteristics of the gayal

- A deadly undead spirit to be found in graveyards and crematoriums.
- Mainly attacks men and pregnant women.

30

GHOUL

The term was introduced to the western world when *One Thousand and One Nights* was first translated into the French language. The European concept of the ghoul is that of a monster that lives in cemeteries and devours corpses. The ghoul is a man-eating supernatural being. They have existed in the Middle East since before the beginning of Islam in the seventh century CE. These demons lurk around graveyards, existing in a state between the living and the dead called the undead. A female ghoul, a ghulah, often referred as Aunt Ghoul or Mother Ghoul, are said to trap lustful men and eat them.

Ghouls sometimes live in the wastelands and take the shape of animals like hyenas. Also known to devour children, they are known to drink blood and steal valuables. These hyena-like ghouls would then take the shape of their most recently consumed human and wander around in the desert, luring more prey towards their den.

The word ghoul, however, is not limited to these monsters. In Arabic, ghoul means a person full of lust and dishonesty.

Interestingly, the term can also refer to people who deal with death, like gravediggers and grave robbers.

Characteristics of the ghoul

- Shape-shifting supernatural creature.
- Encounters with ghouls can be fatal.
- Found throughout the world.

The Book of Indian Dogs

Intestines. Though the term is also used to refer to people who deal with death, say, gravediggers, and grave robbers.

Characteristics of the ghoul
• Shape-shifting supernatural creature
• Encounters with ghouls can be fatal
• Found throughout the world.

31

GUTIYA DEO

Ravi had a feeling that he was in over his head. His problem was that he didn't know how to fix the situation that was threatening to overwhelm him. He and a group of others were travelling in a lorry over a stretch of road in a very poor condition, when right in the middle of a stretch, with no habitation for miles, the vehicle lurched into a deep pothole in the road and could not be extricated. It was a little past midnight; most of his companions were very drunk on cheap Indian-made whisky. When they found themselves marooned in this fashion, after a while they started hunting around for something to keep themselves amused. They decided to pick on Ramdhari, who was often the butt of their jokes and pranks, because he was the shortest member of the group, a little taller than a dwarf really, and therefore, the object of their cruel, insensitive jokes. Ravi, who was the youngest member of the group, would get really angry when Ramdhari was picked on but he didn't have the strength or the seniority to be able to

protect him. And so, he began to fume silently once more when the others began tormenting Ramdhari.

After a while, Ramdhari could take it no longer. He quietly got out of the truck and walked away from them. Not knowing what else to do, Ravi stared towards the tiny figure of his friend, getting smaller with the distance. In a moment, the other members got down from the lorry and poured some water on the surrounding ground, creating a slippery mud. Their drunk selves turned off the street lamp and their cunning eyes began staring at the path, waiting for Ramdhari to return and fall on their trap.

After quite a bit of wait in the darkness of the midnight where the only light was the half-moon, a small human figure, as dark as a shadow, slowly walked towards them. All the eyes stared down to witness the fun. But he did not slip on the mud, he stood there for a moment, sighed and walked away, off the road and towards the forest.

Ravi got out of the lorry as well and followed the tiny figure. The minute he got off the road, his feet began to crackle on the dry leaves that were scattered beneath the tree. Ravi was only a few feet behind and vaguely wondered how he was able to walk soundlessly on this layout of dried leaves. He could hear the other drunken members of the group getting out of the lorry to follow him; they weren't going to let their quarry off so easily. He could see the short figure dimly ahead of them among the trees. He thought it must be a trick of the eye but the figure seemed a bit taller. A few minutes later, the shadowy figure was as tall as the trees of the forest. Suddenly, Ravi was startled by a noise, he looked back and saw Ramdhari standing beside him, as if he woke up from a nap. Ramdhari looked at the drunk crowd and curiously asked,

'What is happening? Where are they going?' And, then, full of awe and terror, Ravi looked back towards the forest—the dwarf had somehow metamorphosed into the tallest tree of the forest. The others had seen it, too. Their drunken chatter stopped as if a tap had been turned off. A thick silence reigned in the forest.

Characteristics of the gutiya deo

- A dwarf ghost.
- Encounters with it are rarely fatal.
- To be found in Bihar.

32

GUYASI

This is a tale from a small town where the inhabitants were proud of their simple lives. They maintained a steady connection with most people who stayed there for a long time and supported each other in their needs.

Mohanlal wanted to take a plunge into the real-estate business. He had calculated the profits of building high-rise apartments in smaller townships, and so, when he heard of this town and the abandoned area in the middle of a popular locality, he tried to get in touch with the owner. This proved difficult since no one seemed to remember where the last owner had disappeared or who had claimed this land after him. He happily made arrangements to clear it up and started taking measurements. This bit was harder since the whole place looked like nobody had cleaned it in ages and people who live nearby kept piling their rubbish on top. Many trees and bushes had overrun the whole area which made the place seem dark even during daytime. Annoyed at the last owner's laziness, Mohanlal hired a few cleaners to start working on the plot.

'You can't clean it. Nobody can clean it,' said an old man standing behind him as Mohanlal waited for the cleaners to arrive at the plot.

'What do you mean you can't clean it? You are just lazy, aren't you? Living with this rubbish around!'

The old man laughed.

'Do you think we never tried? It won't let you.' He disappeared.

Mohanlal was too practical a man to get threatened so easily. Annoyed at the workers for getting late, he grew even more agitated when only one man showed up at midday.

'We can't work here, sir. This place is haunted.' Though he looked frail, his voice was firm. 'We have tales, many tried working here and died. It won't let you breathe'.

'What on earth can stop you from breathing! I get it, the smell is terrible. Get something on your face, like a mask. Charge me extra for that!'

'Don't place anything on your face. It won't let you breathe.'

Without another word he left. Mohanlal was furious. These small-town people never had the courage to try something new. He came back the next day with a few other cleaners he hired from the next town. They gathered around, checked their tools and entered the field. As soon as they stepped in, they ran out of the place.

'We can't work in here. This place is evil'. They didn't wait for an answer and stepped away.

Mohanlal grew mad. He was so furious with the behaviours of these people he walked into the field himself.

The smell was terrible indeed. The deeper he walked through the garbage and the darker areas, the stronger the smell became.

He felt something clutch at his chest. Soon he felt something was pounding away on his chest. He covered his nose with a handkerchief, but it didn't help. Rather, the piece of cloth seemed to block his breath even more. Scared now, he decided to leave. He tried walking faster, but he couldn't. He tried to scream for help but the handkerchief had blocked his breath completely. He fell on the ground, struggling for air.

The next morning his body was found in the corner of the ground with the handkerchief stuck firmly to his face.

Characteristics of the gayasi
- The ghost of dirt and shadows dwells in dark garbage-strewn areas.
- Blocks the respiratory system and chokes its victims to death.
- Very dangerous.

33

HARA

Malati wasn't really nervous when she got married in a village far away from her own. All the other girls of her age got married nearby. She had always been the bold sort. Accepting a good proposal from a faraway village had not seemed daunting. She was one of the prettiest in her group. Her new family was very kind and welcoming to her. She took her new responsibilities seriously, quickly figured out what would be acceptable to her in-laws, and fitted perfectly into her new home.

Being part of a big family and the wife of the richest son, she had few chores to do during the day. She would take dirty utensils to the nearby pond in the afternoon to wash them. If she finished early, she'd sometimes take a swim in the pond. She had learnt swimming from her elder brother, and always found it the best form of relaxation.

One day, when Malati emerged from the pond in her drenched sari, one of the neighbours, a young woman, got very scared. She told her there was a hara ghost in that pond. It stole utensils and

made off with valuable jewellery that was left unattended by the pond. It had even been known to pull the legs of children who ventured into the pond for a swim.

Malati felt like laughing. She had heard of this ghost before. Being a good swimmer, she wasn't intimidated by the story.

She was more concerned about another neighbour whom she could sometimes spot in the bushes, gawking at her as she came out of the pond in wet clothes. She would wrap herself up to cover as much of herself as she could but that didn't really help. That creepy man even came up one day to talk to her directly.

Malati came home fuming. She couldn't imagine someone being so shameless as to make such innuendos to a married woman. Outraged by his audacity, she had slapped his face. He had left wordlessly. Malati did not make a fuss about it. Not wanting to make matters worse, she stayed away from the pond for a few days and made excuses of being sick. But that didn't last forever, and soon she had to go back to the pond.

She took along one of the small girls from the house while washing the dishes and kept looking over her shoulder. Nobody could be seen around the pond. She didn't dare have a bath that day and left. The next few days passed without any incident. Malati was relieved. She convinced herself that the slap had worked, and that creep had given up. She didn't bother the kid any more and started going back again on her own.

She took a bath in the pond the next day. As evening fell, Malati felt the water get colder and decided to get out of the water. Suddenly, she felt a sharp tug on her leg. She panicked and lost her balance. As she swallowed some water and tried getting her head above the surface, she felt someone grab her waist and try to grope her. She wanted to shout, but she was still being pulled under. By then she recognized the neighbour and what his intentions were. The more she struggled to free herself from his clutches, the fiercer his grip on her grew. He was a very good swimmer and relentlessly pulled her deeper. As he dragged her down, he kept running his other hand over her body.

Then, she saw a dark shadow emerge from the bottom of the pond. Even though in the depths of the pond it was very dark, the water seemed to grow darker. The dark shape entwined itself with the body of Malati's tormentor and began dragging him deeper into the pond. Taken aback, he let go of Malati. Now it was his turn to struggle and try hard to get himself free. Malati pulled herself up. As she pulled herself out of the water, she saw the dark shape engulf the man and drag him into the muddy depths of the pond.

Characteristics of the hara

- The ghost lives in the still waters of ponds and lakes.
- Some believe them to be the spectral projections of people who drowned.
- Usually not harmful.
- Can sometimes kill.

34

IFRIT

Ifrits are the spirits of the dead, and they roam around the underworld. Islamic mythology depicts them as evil demons of the jinn family of supernatural creatures. Sly, malicious, and wicked, their position among the jinns is not prominent since they lack powerful supernatural gifts.

The Quran uses 'ifrit' to describe a genre of supernatural creatures. This word was not found in pre-Islamic Arabia.

In the Surah An-Naml, an ifrit describes himself as strong and trustworthy and offers to carry the throne of Bilqis to Solomon. In the hadith of Muhammad al-Bukhari, an ifrit among the jinns is said to have attempted to interrupt the prayers of Prophet Muhammad. In the narratives of Malik ibn-Anas, the archangel Jibreel teaches a du'a to Prophet Muhammad to defeat the ifrits.

The ifrits can be either evil or good. Although they are considered creatures of the underworld, they sometimes serve God's purposes. Most of the time they carry out instructions to wreck blood vengeance and assist in avenging murders. They can be summoned and be bound to serve the purpose of a sorcerer or a summoner.

In Egypt, an ifrit originates as the spirit of someone who has been killed or murdered. These spirits are evil and seek vengeance. They roam around the earth, in graveyards and in places the person frequented when alive.

In Moroccan culture, ifrits are powerful jinns with the ability to possess living beings. They are also depicted as monsters with thorny, clawed hands, flaming eyes, and sometimes even with seven bloody heads.

In the *One Thousand and One Nights*, ifrits are said to possess evil desires and are out to kidnap. They are able to take on the form of different animals.

Characteristics of the ifrit

- Belong to the family of jinns (see chapter 37).
- Are usually evil but can occasionally do the bidding of God.
- Very vengeful.

35

JHAPRI

Mahavir was the most notorious thief in the entire village. It was said that he could steal the pillow or the mattress from beneath a sleeping person and the person wouldn't even know. It was very difficult to catch him during the act as he never left any clues. Many reported him to the zamindar, but he always got away due to lack of evidence. His son was never interested in his father's way of living and started a business to lead a normal life. Mahavir thought he should at least pass on his legacy and when he became older, he gave lessons on thievery to his grandson, Mohan.

By the time Mohan grew up, the village had turned into a town. He found it really difficult to apply his grandfather's techniques because there were usually guards in front of apartments or big shops. Once he tried to steal a tiffin from a fellow student in his school and later found out that the box was already empty. He was caught red-handed when he tried to put the box back. In comparison to his grandfather, he became the most unsuccessful thief ever. After many failed attempts, he made his biggest blunder thus far when he tried to steal a big box he had spotted outside a house. He thought it was a storage for fruits or something, but it turned out to be a very fancy dustbin. Deeply discouraged, he went to see his friends that night and told them his story. Everybody rolled on the floor laughing at him. They kept saying 'Jhapte giye hege chhoray.' (You spread shit while stealing).

Mohan was furious. He knew he had to salvage his reputation. He tried to look into his grandfather's belongings to find something that might help. One of the techniques Mahavir used was disguise. On rare occasions, it came in very handy. Mohan picked out a few items from his grandfather's possessions in preparation for his next attempt.

There were still places in the town with traces of the past. Some old buildings and streets still resembled the old village. As Mr Basu passed through the dark shortcut on his bicycle, something sticky landed on his head and shoulder. It had such a bad odour that he had to stop to wipe it off. As he got off the bicycle, he realized a dark figure wearing a toka (a cone-shaped hat made of dry palm leaves) had jumped down from a nearby tree and was slowly crawling towards him. He shrieked and broke into a run. Smirking, Mohan climbed onto the man's bicycle with his bag still hanging on it, took off the hat and the mask, and cycled home grinning broadly.

Mohan started feeling proud, having successfully stolen a bicycle. He began to have more success. He stole bags full of groceries, vegetables, more bicycles, and one day, he came across a bagful of money. When he came home that night, he found excrement on his toka. This surprised him since he used plastic bags to carry the excrement he would toss on his victims, before robbing them, as he had done with the man on the bicycle; he was careful not to get any excrement on his clothes. He cleaned it, reminding himself to be more careful.

The next evening, he perched himself on a low branch of a tree, waiting for someone with a bag to pass by. Soon, he spotted someone dragging a heavy sack possibly filled with their monthly groceries. Mohan kept his bag of shit ready. Just then, something sticky landed on his hat and started dripping over the brim. The odour was so terrible he had to take the hat off. He looked up and saw a dark figure on the upper branch of the tree. The toka on its head was glistening, but the rest of its face was so shadowy he could scarcely make anything out.

The traveller on the road with the heavy bag was startled to see a figure leap out of a tree, and ran away as if all the hounds of heaven were after him.

Characteristics of the jhapri

- Lives on trees.
- A ghost that shits on people.
- Wears a toka.
- Free spirit.
- Not really fatal, but scares and disturbs people.
- Found in Bengal.

36

JILAIYA

Nobody really cares about the bride's wishes in a traditional household, and Urmila was no exception. Every time she asked for something for the wedding, she was told to ask her future husband, Brijesh. After the wedding, she was hugely frustrated at being unable to get herself a pet bird for company. When her husband said that her mother-in-law did not like birds, she felt even worse. This was how the conflict between Urmila, and her mother-in-law, Leela Devi, started. And it wouldn't let up. They would begin fighting early in the morning, and Brijesh took to leaving early for work to get some peace of mind.

He was terrified of having to pick sides when his wife and mother argued. Ever since Urmila had become pregnant, she was even more aggressive, which made it harder for him to calm the waters.

To soothe her unfulfilled desire, Urmila would feed the birds on the roof. These birds would then perch on the tree in the courtyard. Whenever Urmila and her mother-in-law fought,

the first thing Leela Devi would do was shoo the birds away. This morning was no exception. As soon as Brijesh left, she shooed the birds away, complaining that they dirtied the courtyard. At dusk, Leela Devi rudely shooed one bird who didn't seem to care and kept circling the open courtyard. Angrily, she started throwing small objects at it.

Urmila lost her temper. By custom, she wasn't allowed to take her mother-in-law's name, so she called her 'Brijesh ki mummy' or, Brijesh's mother. She screamed at 'Brijesh ki mummy' to leave the bird alone. Leela Devi retorted, calling Urmila the most shameless woman she had ever met.

That day, everybody knew the fight had gone too far. They waited for the next morning for things to settle down.

In the morning, Brijesh was found lying in his bed motionless. There was a deep gash on his throat, which was bleeding profusely.

The terrifying scene shocked everyone into silence. The two women stopped fighting immediately. After Brijesh was cremated, they continued to live in the silent house, taking great care to avoid each other. Urmila even gave up on feeding the birds or asking for one. She would spend the days in her room, or sometimes go up to the rooftop and stand alone for hours.

One afternoon she saw a bird circling the roof again. Maybe from the way it was circling—or perhaps the unease she felt by the way it cast a shadow on her even in the light of day—she could tell it was the same bird that had caused the fight the day before Brijesh had died. She tried to shoo it away. This time it left without much trouble.

When Urmila gave birth to a frail baby, Leela Devi completely lost her mind. She believed someone had cursed her family. Urmila spent all day in bed, weeping. Every evening, Leela Devi would shout at the top of her voice: 'These monsters, again! You know what, Urmila? I'll kill them all!'

One evening, hearing an unholy racket Urmila came out of her room to find her mother-in-law throwing whatever was within her reach at the birds sitting on the branches of nearby trees, and circling overhead. 'Demons, Urmila, demons. They must all be killed,' she screamed. As she looked around, Urmila shrieked when she saw a familiar bird perched on a branch, its malevolent gaze fixed upon her. Hastily averting her eyes, she went to her room and locked the door.

The next morning, Leela Devi had to break the door open when Urmila didn't respond to her name being called. She knocked open the door to find Urmila lying in her bed. Her throat was slit open, still dripping blood.

Characteristics of the jilaiya

- A bird ghost.
- Kills the person it hears the name of, by slitting their throat.
- If its shadow falls on a pregnant woman, they will give birth to weaklings.
- Stories about them come from the villages of Bihar.

37

JINN

We all have heard about the wish-granting spirits, famously known by their anglicized name, 'genies'. These spirits are said to have originated from early pre-Islamic Arabian countries, where they were known as jinns. They began to appear in Islamic myth, scripture and folklore, and men who travelled to India and other parts of Asia carried these stories with them..They are born neither good nor evil, choosing their nature as they grow old.

A plural cognitive noun, the singular form of the term is 'jinni'. It relates to 'majnun', meaning possessed, and is also thought to be derived from 'jannah', meaning the heaven, and 'janin', meaning the embryo. Though the origin of term is contested, some say it arose from the word 'genie' in the eighteenth-century French translation of *One Thousand and One Nights*.

In Islamic religious texts, the jinn is generally characterized as any supernatural spirit, often mentioned together with the Shaitan or the Devil. Alternatively, in Islamic folklore, they are described as supportive and helpful beings in folk tales, and their magical powers are known all over the world.

In pre-Islamic Arabia, jinns were worshipped as they were believed to cause mental and physical illnesses as well as storms. They were never considered equal to gods as they were thought to be mortal beings; they lived in dark places and people had to protect themselves from these supernatural beings.

Just like angels and demons, they are believed to be undetectable by human senses and to have roamed the earth before Adam was created. They eat, drink, reproduce, and after death, just like humans, are sent to heaven or hell depending on their deeds.

As Islam spread across Iran, Africa, Turkey, and India, the concept of jinn mixed with local beliefs about supernatural entities.

They are believed to appear as both humans and animals. In the human form, they are mostly invisible. Sometimes they can also take the form of wind, mists, sandstorms, and shadows. They can change shape at will.

Characteristics of the jinn
- A very powerful supernatural being.
- Can become good or evil depending upon the nature of its deeds.
- Found mainly in the Middle East but also in many parts of Asia.

38

KALPURUSH

The term 'kalpurush' in Bengali usually refers to the constellation, Orion. Its connected dots look like a hunter with his bow, and in some cultures, the god of death.

Since it is a kind of male succubus, let us first talk about what succubi usually are. In order to explain wet dreams, people came up with the excellent idea of blaming it on a ghost. The succubus, predominantly female, is a kind of spirit that shows up in the dead of night and enters a man's dreams. It would then proceed to seduce its victim and engage in sexual intercourse. The male form, kalpurush, is born when a man dies before marriage. They are shape-shifters and can be found lurking in the darkness or hiding in closets or just sitting beside attractive women. They are masters at seducing women.

There are many recorded claims of sightings of the kalpurush. Wandering around, it can be recognized by two unusually long arms, a hunched body, and burning bright eyes that glow in the dark. The women who encounter the kalpurush are said to develop two symptoms immediately. First, they run a high fever and then they start speaking gibberish. Some women are also said to lose their minds completely and do inexplicable things. In Bengali, the word 'kalpurush' is dervied from 'kal' meaning death and 'purush' meaning a male.

Characteristics of the kalpurush
- Male version of the succubus.
- Is notorious for preying on women.
- Rarely deadly.

39

KANAVULO

Mrinal had been asked to inspect a school located in Purulia district. It would take him a day to do the job and he would return the same day. He was the only one who got off the train at the deserted station. Kapil, a member of the school staff, was waiting at the station. Purulia had always fascinated Mrinal—its flaming palash trees, dry, red soil, and calm vastness. On this visit, though, sitting on the back of Kapil's motorcycle, he was disappointed by what he saw—stubbled fields after the harvest, no trace of the stretching colour in the landscape they drove through.

Kapil made slow progress, taking a left or right turn occasionally. The journey shouldn't have taken more than ten minutes, but they were slowed down by the bumpy village path. The school was at the entrance of the village. It was small yet clean and tidy. The inspection, though formal, was not very time-consuming. The headmaster's office looked organized and everything went smoothly except for one glitch. There was a report of an order for fifty books, which were missing from their library. A simple case of misuse of funds, which wasn't uncommon in Mrinal's experience. But the staff insisted one of them was coming back with the shipment shortly. The order had been placed almost a month ago, so their logic seemed feeble to Mrinal. He made a note in his report and finished his work by midday.

Delighted to have finished early, he decided to walk to the station to enjoy the village surroundings. When he told Kapil, the man seemed uncomfortable, possibly anxious he would lose his way, Mrinal thought. He was amused by Kapil's concern and had no hesitation in turning down his offer for a ride. He had travelled over 150 kilometres to get here and the one-kilometre walk to the station would give him no trouble whatsoever. He wanted to catch the next train at 2.30 p.m. and started walking down the path forty-five minutes earlier. People probably came here a lot since there were markings on the electricity poles, made with mud and stones. One said 'Suman'. A funny habit people had, putting their names in all sorts of places. He couldn't see the village any more and laughed at 'Suman' for coming all the way here to inscribe his name on a pole.

A short while later, Mrinal couldn't deny feeling a tiny bit of regret at having refused Kapil's offer. What seemed like ten minutes on the motorbike was now making him feel exhausted. He increased his pace since it was almost time for the train's departure. He had accepted by then that he would miss this train and would now have to wait for another two hours for the next one. He thought of returning to the school but walking back the whole distance wasn't an appealing idea either. He decided to keep going towards the station. There was no sign of the railway track, neither could he hear the 2.30 p.m. train pass by. Hoping that the train was late, he wondered if he could still make it and increased his pace to a light jog. Another half an hour passed and there was still no sign of the station. By now he was panting and leaned on the nearest pole to catch his breath. The mud on the pole was making his sweaty palms slip. He looked at the pole, annoyed, to realize he had just wiped off half of 'Suman' from it. He felt panic take over. He had clearly lost his way. He hoped that he had accidentally come closer to the village again, which meant he could ask Kapil to drop him off this time. So, he walked for another hour, but there was no village in sight. Unable to walk any more, the panic in his heart spiralled when he spotted the partially erased 'Suman' sign again. He started running now. Shouting, calling for help. If anybody was passing through these fields, they might hear him. It was almost dusk, and he knew that after darkness fell, he would not be able to get out of these fields until morning. He could hardly see where he was going. It didn't matter anyway since everywhere he turned looked exactly the same. He tripped on something and passed out. When he came to his senses he saw what was blocking his way. It was a bag with something heavy inside. He looked inside. There were around forty to fifty books. Some of them were open, their pages ripped out. Somebody had mercilessly torn random pages from the books and left them lying here. He felt a tingle run up his spine. There was something odd about this whole place. He wanted to run, get away as far as he could. But his legs were paralysed, he couldn't move an inch.

'Did you find the way?' A frail-looking man, with eyes that bulged out, was standing in front of him.

'The way to where?' he managed to say.

'Anywhere.' he said. 'You can take a few pages from the books if you are hungry.'

He sounded mad. Mrinal tried to calm him down.

'H–how long have you been looking for the way?'

'Not sure, may be a month, a year. I was supposed to go to the school with this shipment. Kept my name written on a pole, thinking it would help me find the way. But it won't let you out; it'll never let you out.'

'W–what won't let me out?'

'Can't you feel it? It'll make you lose your way forever.'

Terrified now, Mrinal started running madly again. Weakly, the figure shouted, 'If you see my name written on a pole, keep walking right from there.'

He didn't know what was to the right or what was to the left of him. He kept running blindly. The last thing he remembered when he bumped into the pole were the partially erased letters '...man', vaguely visible in the darkness.

Characteristics of the kanavulo

- Make people lose their way.
- Lives in abandoned meadows.
- Encounters with it can be fatal.
- Found in Purulia district, Bengal.

40

KANIPISHACHI

The woman was back again. Moni was on the verge of tears when her mother-in-law gave away her favourite sari that her husband had gifted her on their anniversary. She knew this would happen when she had burned a minuscule hole in her sari while ironing that morning. She tried to convince everyone that she could easily hide the burn hole inside the folds of the sari, but all in vain. Unerringly, the dark, thin figure knocked on their door the next evening and her mother-in-law hastily gave the sari to her in no time. Oh, how Moni despised the sight of that veiled woman standing in their courtyard!

She tried to convince her husband that his mother was being fooled and that the veiled woman was making good money selling the expensive clothes with tiny defects that her mother-in-law was blithely giving away. Her husband, who was used to this custom, paid her no heed, which bothered her even more.

Moni sometimes spotted the veiled woman washing the clothes she had received from their house in the local pond during the evening. She became convinced that the woman was deceiving them. Everything about her repelled Moni. She had to find a way to stop her mother-in-law from giving away their clothes to her. As a result, she became obsessed with not damaging her belongings. She washed and ironed each piece of garment herself to keep them intact. When her son, Rabin, was born, she gave him lessons on how to keep his clothes in a good condition. Years passed and nobody saw that woman again at their door. But, Moni's obsession remained, making everyone take good care of their clothes.

Rabin usually kept himself away from brawls and disputes in his school. But, one day, when his best friend, Raju, was attacked by the senior boys, he had to intervene. In the process, his shirt was torn. The red and white checked shirt was a part of a brand-new uniform that he had got after being promoted to the new class. Rabin knew his mother would be furious. He mentioned this to Raju, who came up with a solution. He collected a safety pin and pinned the torn area together. If Rabin kept his hands crossed the tear wouldn't show.

Rabin was pleased when his mother didn't notice the damage right away. However, he knew she'd wash the shirt in a few days, and he would face her wrath then. He was pretending to study when he heard a loud commotion outside. His mother was shouting at a woman standing in the courtyard—a thin veiled figure. Moni couldn't sleep that night. She didn't know why the sight of that woman disturbed her after all these years. When Moni said they didn't have anything to give away, she left without a word. Still, she couldn't get the uneasy feeling out of her head.

Rabin spent the next day feeling anxious. He was wondering how to explain the tear to his mother. On top of that, he saw a veiled woman in the corner of their school courtyard when he got to school in the morning. He had a strange feeling that she had visited their home last night as well. He had even spotted a similar figure from the window of his class, lurking in the corner of the school playground. Raju, who was trying to catch his attention, was disappointed when he discovered the source of Rabin's distraction.

Rabin knew he was being followed on his way back home. A short while later, a familiar figure was blocking his path. But she wasn't veiled any more.

Moni too had been feeling troubled the whole day. She couldn't get any work done. So, she kept walking around the pond behind their house until dusk.

As night fell, the woman was back again. A dark thin figure with a pile of clothes. Moni shuddered when she spotted a familiar red checked shirt being washed. She ran back to the house only to find out Rabin had never made it home.

Characteristics of the kanipishachi

- Female ghost.
- Washes torn clothes in a pond every evening.
- Kills people who wear torn clothes.
- Found in Bengal.

41

KHABISH

Certain kinds of zombies, known as khabish, are scattered across the Himalaya. The reason they are often termed as zombies is because of the way they are formed. Unlike most other ghosts, no one has to die to become a khabish. A khabhish can begin to seep into a human being, usually a middle-aged man and start the metamorphosis. Gradually their prey transforms into a khabish.

A khabish usually has the following distinctive features: a missing right arm and pustules all over its skin. It has poor eyesight and is often prone to chest pain and tremors. It often looks sleepy.

A khabish can be spotted from a distance since it shouts curses at people it sees. It is said that if someone wanders in the Himalaya at night, they might hear someone shouting obscene words at them in a hoarse voice. If they pinpoint the source of the voice, they might spot an armless, rotting figure with breathing issues and blisters all over the body. If they make eye contact, the observer, too, will turn into a khabish.

A story of two travellers accompanies the tale of khabish.

The two men, while indulging in night photography, spotted an armless figure in the wild. One of them got so annoyed by the abuses he was hurling at them that he threw stones at it and made eye contact with the creature. On their way back, he too started uttering curse words. Later that night, rashes started erupting on his skin. His friend thought it was some kind of allergy common in the mountains. Even the difficulty he had seeing seemed to be a result of allergic fevers. But once the chest pain started and the rashes turned into grotesque blisters, they decided to consult a doctor in the morning. The whole night, the infected traveller stood in front of his friend's closed door and shouted abuses at him. His voice grew hoarser as the night went on. By morning the man inside the room heard a thud outside the door and the sound of heavy footsteps walking away. After a while he opened the door to see the right arm of his friend lying on the ground with the watch around the wrist still ticking.

Characteristics of the khabish

- A form of zombie.
- Enters the body of a living human being and transforms him into a khabish.
- Usually missing a right arm.
- Found in the Himalaya.

42

KICHIN

Ever since his brother brought home his bride, Saroj had been lusting after his beautiful sister-in-law, Parul. He would stare at her as unobtrusively as he could, drooling over every corner of her luscious body and beautiful face; he would try and engage her in conversation and brush against her by 'accident' whenever he found an opportunity. One day, when he knew she was going to have a bath, he sneaked out of the house, ran around to the room where the window of the bathroom was, dragged a large stone over so he could stand on it, and peeped in. To his unbridled excitement he was able to see Parul undressing and pouring water over her fair skin. Aroused from the sight, and being unable to control his excitement, he rushed off to his room.

While he was laying with his eyes closed, romanticizing the sight in his mind, the cleaning woman, Meena, came in. In his haste, Saroj had forgotten to lock the door. Meena looked at him, and his arousal in the throes of pain, with a vacant stare. Opening his eyes, Saroj caught the maid staring at him, and with a suppressed expletive, he leapt up from the bed and scurried out of the room. The sight of Meena had always repulsed him, he never felt so disgusted seeing anybody else.

Over the next few days, he continued to spy on his sister-in-law through the bathroom window and fantasized about her. He was relieved he hadn't yet been caught, but after a while he began thinking she knew he was spying on her but was egging him on because his brother wasn't sexually fulfilling her. He decided to put his theory to test. The next day, soon after Parul had her bath, he went up to her and looked at her appreciatively. She glanced at him and then went into her bedroom. His brother was away at work, so he decided to hang around his sister-in-law's room, keeping an eye on the closed door. A short while later, it opened, and he was admitted inside, only to see her heading to her bathroom with a fresh towel. Was his theory correct? Did she want him to ogle at her luscious body again? He slunk away to his vantage point and watched her undress. Suddenly, she turned and looked at the window and caught him gaping at her. Her mouth fell open; she swiftly closed the window and hung her spare towel on it.

She then began avoiding him, and a week later announced that she was going to her parents' home. Saroj couldn't have been more frustrated. Thereafter, he would pace up and down the backyard at all times, cursing his luck.

About a week later, as he was reluctantly walking up and down, he heard the sound of familiar footsteps. To his great joy, he saw the woman of his fantasies, Parul boudi walk into the backyard. She said she didn't like it at her at her parents' house and had decided to cut her visit short. The invitation was clear. Saroj ran over to her and dragged her to his bedroom. Saroj forced himself on her, but she didn't put up much resistance either and even seemed to enjoy him making love to her. He climaxed and shut his eyes in ecstasy. When he opened them, he found he was not lying next to Parul but the gross, ugly body of Meena. Saroj felt like puking and jumped out of the bed. Meena rose and started crawling towards him, with hungry eyes, wide open, fixated on his genitals, and a lusty tongue, sticking out, dripping with desire.

Characteristics of the kichin
- Female ghost.
- Seduces men and steals their semen.
- Not fatal.
- Found in Bihar.

43

KOLLIVAI PISAASU

One of the most commonly sighted ghosts in Tamil Nadu, is the kollivai pisaasu or kollivayup pey. These types of ghosts emerge suddenly from the depths of the earth as a flash of light, and disappear just as quickly before the human eye can fathom their existence. People claim to have sighted them in muddy fields, graveyards, and garbage dumps.

The appearance of these pisaasus is said to be ugly and fierce. They have black skin with protruding red veins and big, bright red eyes. They communicate in a distinct language—Paisachi—and are endowed with the power of mind-control and possession.

The kollivai pisaasus coexist with vetal, bhoota, and other evil supernatural creatures around crematoriums, graveyards, and deserted fields. They can take the shapes of humans or animals and dissolve into thin air instantly. Anyone who crosses paths with a pisaasu will die or meet with extremely bad luck or be driven to insanity. There are certain religious rituals which can be performed to get rid of or prevent a pisaasu's possession.

They are known by various names throughout the world: in Bengali, they are called aaleya; in the UK, they are called will-o'-the-wisp. A prosaic scientific explanation for the phenomenon of pisaasus is this: certain bacteria that help in the decomposition of animal and plant remains generate a mixture of combustible gases such as methane and diphosphane. These gases are trapped underground until they are released in the air; upon exposure, they burst into flames.

The sudden burst of light caused by the release of gases shocks people into imagining these ghosts. Interestingly, thanks to our scientific-minded ancestors, the word 'kollivai', or 'kolli-vayu', literally means 'combustible deadly gas'.

Characteristics of the kollivai pisaasu
- A very common spirit.
- Extremely malevolent.
- Found in Tamil Nadu.

44

KUTTI CHAATHAN

Some sources claim kutti chaathan or kutti chetan ghosts spring from people who have died tragic or unnatural deaths. However, most sources characterize them as independent, interdimensional beings with supernatural powers and abilities. These creatures are usually invisible to the human eye, but they can be invoked through certain rituals. They are summoned for specific tasks, and their services can be availed by the exchange of either blood, or money, or both.

Like the evil jinns in *One Thousand and One Nights*, they are reputed to kill and devour the summoner if they are not offered a task worthy of their powers. Moreover, if the summoner fails to recompense the ghost after the completion of the task, they will be tortured until death.

In parts of South India, like Kerala, the kutti chetan is worshipped as a guardian angel, and jewellers summon them to protect their shops from robbers and thieves.

Some paranormal experts have drawn connections between

the kutti chaathan and the noisy German ghost, the poltergeist. References to poltergeists are littered in the folklore of India, Japan, Brazil, Australia, the US, and many European nations. Attention-seekers by nature, they are not commonly killers, but can cause a tremendous nuisance by throwing objects, creating a ruckus, knocking on doors and pinching, biting, and hitting people, all while staying invisible.

The kutti chaathan cannot be destroyed by regular religious procedures undertaken for ghosts because they have not risen from human souls.

Characteristics of the kutti chaathan
- A very commonly found ghost.
- Reputed to be an interdimensional phantom.
- Can be a nuisance and occasionally deadly.
- Can also be benevolent.
- Found in Kerala.

45

MALANDU

Evening arrives on the Western Ghats on the wings of the birds returning to roost. The greenish-dark mountain range echoes in the wind. Far away, the dwindling of the light signals the end of another day.

From the top of a hill, a ghost named malandu watches children playing. The children have been told to return home before 6 p.m. or else the malandu will take down their names. The malandu is said to arrive at nightfall on a white horse and abduct mischievous children. Naturally, the children always come back home on time and don't come out to the streets once evening falls. At night-time, while telling stories to the children, their guardians describe this ghost as having a big moustache, long hair, and wearing boots. If a child returns home in the evening, he or she can hear and see the horse galloping towards them through the window.

This is a tale from Coimbatore in which a child sees a rider coming towards him on a horse. Scared out of his wits, he realizes it is a robber who is carrying a gun. Ready to wake his father, he sees the real horse rider seize the robber from his horse. Just as the horse rider is about to disappear, his head revolves a full 360 degrees towards the child, and with reddish eyes, he shouts at him to fall asleep.

Characteristics of the malandu

- A ghost who kidnaps disobedient children, especially those who stay out late.
- Found in South India.

46

MAMDO

Kritch...kritch...kritch....

Was someone digging up the ground again? Sudhir kept his eyes closed for a while, trying to focus on the sound. He walked up to the front window and drew back the curtain slowly. The street in front of his house looked empty. He scrutinized the field as far as his eyes could reach, but nothing specific showed up. Shutting his eyes again, he tried to identify the direction where the sound was coming from. Maybe it was coming from the other side of the house. That made Sudhir a bit uneasy, since he believed that all bad things transpired on the burial ground on the other side of the road.

But he didn't want to bring up this concern in front of his wife. Their argument about buying a plot and building a house right in front of a burial ground had been going on for two years now. Sudhir had known this was the cheapest deal he was getting at that time. People avoided plots in this well-developed neighbourhood just because of the burial ground. If they could just get the superstitions out of their head, they would realize how profitable this plan was. While persuading his wife, Sudhir had bought a much larger plot than his initial plan and had started the construction of the house. When his wife entered the large hall and the massive garden behind, she was eventually pleased. They had been living a happy life until a couple of weeks ago.

Once in a while, a procession of mourners would come from the nearby Muslim quarter to the burial ground to pay respects to someone who had passed away. Sudhir would watch the whole process from his balcony. Gradually, this became a habit and sometimes, even late at night, after finishing the day's work, he would go to the balcony and stare at the ground for hours. Perhaps the tranquillity of this area eased some of his stress from work. However, the peace didn't last long. A few weeks ago, a street dog was discovered in their garden trying to eat something foul-smelling. Once they realized it was a half-rotten hand of a corpse, his wife started screaming and his son ran inside the house out of fear. This was the first time Sudhir regretted staying close to a burial ground. He disposed of the rotten hand in the nearby pond.

He spent hours trying to spot the half-dug grave from which the dog had got hold of the hand. He knew his obsession was growing stronger when he started hearing the sound of digging even in the middle of the night. Unable to contain his curiosity, one night, he stepped out onto his balcony to investigate. And, there sat a man beside a grave, digging away. He immediately realized what was going on. The person in white clothes and wearing a visible fez was digging out corpses from the graves. Sudhir was aware of the corpse-stealing that went on in burial grounds. Taking a torch from his room, he walked straight down towards the ground. There was nobody there, but he could still see the freshly dug soil over the grave that he had seen from his balcony. He waited for the sound again, but it seemed to be coming from the back of his house. What could the corpse thief be doing at the back of his house?

Reluctantly, he gathered courage and decided to keep an eye on the graveyard the next night. Choosing a suitable hiding spot, he waited for the opportune moment. Perhaps sitting made him a little drowsy, because when he woke up, he saw the same man, with half of his body inside a grave. He looked closely: the man didn't seem to be digging, rather, he was digging himself out. Sudhir was confused. Why would anybody dig themselves out of a grave? What was he doing inside in the first place? Sitting still, Sudhir tried to get another look at the man. It was a full-moon night and once the tall, thin figure clad in all white was out of the grave it moved slowly away. One of the sleeves of its shirt was empty and swayed in the breeze.

Sudhir started sweating. He realized what he had just seen. He walked a few steps towards the grave to make sure. As he expected, it was empty. The man wasn't digging a corpse out, he was digging himself out of the grave.

Suddenly, he heard a small crack behind his back; he became aware somebody was standing right behind him. Sudhir slowly turned around to see a fleshless face with two empty eye sockets boring into him. The last thing he felt was one of his arms being torn from his body before he was thrown into the open grave and buried.

Characteristics of the mamdo

- Very fatal, causes death when encountered.
- The body is just the human skeleton form. Can sometimes be covered in white cloth in which they were buried.
- Wears a fez.

47

MARID

India, the land of 'unity in diversity', is also home to a diverse spectrum of ghosts and spirits. Though marids do not actually originate in India, they have travelled through Islamic culture into Indian ghost lore. The word 'marid' in Arabic translates to 'rebellious'. Another name for this spirit is 'ifrit', that has been described earlier in this book. A supernatural being, marids are considered a type of Shaitan (or Satan), as described in the Quran (37:7). In other sources, the word has been translated to 'demon' and 'giant' and sometimes they are attributed to be the most evil among the genies[*].

In modern references, marids are depicted very differently. In the *Bartimaeus Sequence*, a series of children's novels of alternate history, fantasy, and magic, Jonathan Stroud describes marids as powerful demons that can be summoned by magicians. In the *Daevabad Trilogy* by S. A. Chakraborty, or the popular boardgame Dungeons

---

[*]Ibn Manzur, *Lisan al-Arab*, Lebanon: Dar Sader, p. 5 and 376.

& Dragons, marids are described as aquatic supernatural creatures.

Marids are described vividly in the Hadith. In one of the stories, an ifrit tries to attack Prophet Muhammad using fire-bolts. They are also said to shape-shift into animals.

Marids usually concern themselves with kings and holy people, unlike other genies, who engage with commoners.

Characteristics of the marid

- Originated in Arabia.
- Another name for them is 'ifrit'.
- A form of jinn.
- Found all across the world.

48

MASAN

'You have to see these! This year is mine, baby!'

Sagar came to the room, almost screaming. He looked tired and pale. Yet, his eyes were glittering from the excitement. 'Didn't I tell you, honey? Misty mountains are much more dazzling than other landscapes. I'll show you...call the others!'

Prakash and Mihir came to the room, equally excited. Although they didn't share the same level of enthusiasm as Sagar when it came to photography, they were accompanying him on this trip to Shimla with their families for the sake of adventure. They spent two days wandering around the area, and all of them took marvellous photographs of the mountainscape. As the weather turned cloudy, Sagar went off on his own on a motorbike that he had borrowed from the landlord of their homestay to take photographs to his heart's content. Now, he wanted to show the family his pictures.

Rina, his wife, made space in the room for others to join in. The projector had been readied for everyone to get a better look. Rina took Avi into her lap. Their son got very excited every time

Sagar had his projector on. It reminded him of when they watched movies together—one of Avi's favourite ways to spend time with his father. He also knew a lot about photography, much more than was appropriate for a five-year-old, in Rina's opinion. In short, he loved his father's job!

The pictures were fascinating, indeed. Mountain ranges framed against blue skies and covered with forests...you could never have enough of these. Every slide was followed by a sense of awe and often gasps of admiration. Rina could sense Sagar's excitement looking at the awestruck faces.

Suddenly, a high-pitched scream pierced the silence. It was Avi. He screamed so suddenly and so loudly that everyone jumped to their feet. He wasn't smiling any more. His cheeks were red and eyes wide open; he was clearly reacting to the picture projected on the wall right now. It looked like a normal valley with scattered trees here and there with nothing extraordinary. But Avi kept screaming and struggling on his mother's lap as if he wanted to leave the room. Oblivious to everyone's attempts to calm him down, the frightened child kept looking at the picture and screaming.

Uneasily, Sagar turned the projector off. Avi was now sobbing into his father's chest, asking to take him home right away. They still had two days left of their trip and nobody understood what could have disturbed the child. They all made vain attempts to distract him from crying, but Avi refused to eat anything at dinner and didn't stop crying all night.

Early the next morning, they were extremely worried since Avi was still sobbing. Looking at his red face and puffy eyes, they wondered if he had imagined something scary in the foggy picture. They decided to take him to see the place, show him around, in

the hope that he would calm down. They called for three cars and Sagar gave the drivers directions to the place. The whole time, Avi kept crying harder and pleading that he didn't want to go. But, to everyone's relief, as soon as they arrived, he stopped crying. They all stepped out of the car happily and started walking around. Just then, one of the drivers pulled Sagar aside.

'Why here, sir?'

'What do you mean?'

'This used to be a charnel ground, sir. Please don't take anything home from here. It's an evil place.'

Sagar grew nervous. He told the others about the conversation which fascinated them even more. Cameras out, they started taking photographs of the area. A veil of mist had descended. Rina, too, was relieved and walked around with everyone. Then, they lost sight of Avi. Panic broke as everyone searched for the boy frantically, but there was no trace of Avi. They asked the drivers of the three cars that had transported them there, but they hadn't seen the child leave the area.

They kept searching till darkness fell, then decided to inform the police. Although it was impossible to drag Rina away from the spot, they had to decide what to do next. 'The pictures!' Prakash said. 'We took many pictures, right? He must be in some of the pictures; let's try to trace which way he went!'

Once everyone agreed, they put together all of the pictures to get a better view on Sagar's projector. In the few pictures where Avi was visible in the background, he was looking up with a dark shadow hovering over his head. In the next photograph, it was almost touching his head. In the subsequent picture, the shadow had formed a circle around his head. In the final slide, half of his body had been consumed by the shadow.

Characteristics of the masan
- Spirit which preys on children.
- Found in burial grounds.
- Can take the shape of a cloud.
- Found in the Himalayan valley.
- When a lower-caste person dies and their bodies are left half burnt in the charnel ground, they haunt that ground as the masan ghost.

49

MECHHO BHOOT

Parimal knew something was up the moment he stepped into the shabby office. After two decades of service, he could tell when people were being untruthful just by looking at them. This was his fifth transfer in the last ten years as an officer-in-charge in a large company that traded in seafood and freshwater fish with offices all over the country. Parimal was single and middle-aged and didn't mind being transferred frequently but this time he was sure that something was wrong. Everyone was vague about why his predecessor had quit, and there was a lot that didn't seem right with the functioning of this office.

He noticed many gaps in the reports of collection and export. On counting the daily number of fish types, he observed that the export numbers did not match the records. He threatened his workers, imposed fines, and even suspended a few of those whom he suspected, but nothing changed. They came up with the most unique excuse for the shortage—they claimed it was the handiwork of the mechho bhoot, a spirit that steals fish! They even went on to specify that one of the fishers named Kanai Das who had died while catching fishes in the dam haunted the warehouse and ate the fish.

Parimal was not going to give up that easily. He doubled the guards at the storage unit but he couldn't stop the disappearance of the fish. Sometimes he'd walk quietly in the vicinity of the warehouse with a stick in his hand. He even made surprise checks on the houses of the workers, all of whom stayed nearby, to see if he could trace where the fish were going. He started sniffing the bags everyone carried in and out of the workplace. The more he harassed the workers, the more everyone blamed Kanai Das. Parimal suspended two of his subordinates and decided to stake out the warehouse that night.

He would catch the thief in the act and prove everyone in the office was lying. He kept the place open in the evening, and sneaked past the guards into the warehouse. As the night wore on, he could hear the guards laughing and chatting outside, but inside, all was quiet. In the early hours of the morning, he saw him. The dark thin figure of the thief was sliding in through the window. The man crawled onto a heap of boxes and opened one.

With a shout, Parimal rushed towards him. Startled, the figure disappeared through the window. Parimal followed. With no time to call the others, Parimal kept his eyes on the dark figure, who was now crossing the field next to the warehouse. He ran steadily onwards until he reached the main road.

The disappearance of the officer-in-charge for almost a week was surprising, yet a relief for everyone else at the fishery office. They filed a missing person's report and soon returned to their normal routine. One of the guards tried to tell the other that he had heard a commotion in the warehouse the day Parimal had disappeared, but nobody paid much attention to his report. Then, a week later, the guard heard a noise inside the warehouse. When he went inside and shone his torch on the source of the noise, he was dumbstruck to see his former boss. Eyes glazed and fixed on nothing in particular, Parimal reached into the box he had torn open, pulled out a raw fish, ripped off its head and began crunching on its bones.

Characteristics of the mechho bhoot

- If a person obsessed with fish dies they could become a mechho bhoot.
- Steals and eats fish.
- Usually not fatal if allowed to eat its share of the catch.

50

MOHINI

The word mohini originates from a Sanskrit shloka, 'mayam ashito mohinim', which describes one of the avatars of Lord Vishnu. The mohini is the epitome of female beauty; she is the only one who could distract Mahadev.

The mohini was first introduced in the Mahabharata, when the asuras tried to take away the elixir of immorality, amrita, without letting the gods have their fair share. Vishnu took the shape of this femme fatale and proceeded to grab the attention of all the asuras and ultimately, she took away the pot of amrita. When mohini distributed the amrita among the gods, an asura named Rahu, in disguise, took a share. Chandra and Surya, the moon and the sun gods, identified and informed Vishnu, who cut off Rahu's head; however, the elixir had travelled to his throat by that time, leaving the head immortal. Rahu's head still wanders around in space, trying to devour the sun and the moon, and this action causes the lunar and solar eclipses.

The ghost called mohini is often depicted as a beautiful woman with shiny, long hair. Sometimes she holds a baby in her arms and walks the streets at night. If unsuspecting drivers stop to offer help or a ride, the spirit will get into the car repeating the word 'mohini'. The drivers would later be found either half-mad or completely insane.

Characteristics of the mohini

- Divine temptress, an avatar of Lord Vishnu.
- Extraordinarily beautiful to look at.
- Drives its victims insane.
- Found in South India.

51

MUNCHOWA

'The new face of our brand is Meenakshi!'

Meenakshi had seen the video clip at least twenty times since the evening. She couldn't get enough of the calls and messages that had flooded her inbox. She left the auditorium right after the gala dinner and it was just past midnight now. She continued replying to all the celebrities who congratulated her for signing on as the new model of a famous brand. She knew this was a trick of the trade. She had to stay in touch with the right people at the right time.

Watching the skyline from her rooftop had always been one of her favourite things to do. Looking at the horizon stretching from one end of the city to the other was like watching her dream expand beyond Kanpur. Now that she was the top model in the city, she needed to think about moving to Mumbai. When she had moved to her present apartment after the owner of the biggest modelling agency gifted it to her, she knew her life was going to change soon. All she had to do was to wipe off her middle-class inhibitions and adapt to the industry's ways.

She closed her eyes and felt the fresh air on her face. The air was cold, probably colder than usual. She felt a shiver and smiled. She often shivered when the big banners flashing her face lit up the entire auditorium. She decided to watch the video clip again. She picked up her cell phone, but it didn't unlock with the face recognition feature. She smiled again. Now that the whole city recognized her face, why was her phone was refusing to do so? She unlocked it using the passcode and started watching the clip again, lighting up a cigarette. The flame from the lighter felt too hot on her face. Or maybe the cold air had made her skin too sensitive. She kept watching the clips.

Was she catching a fever now? Her body felt the chill in the cold air around her, but her face still felt like it was burning. She had her first shoot the next day and it wouldn't do to fall sick! She decided to go downstairs and get some medicines.

'The face of the town, eh! Enjoying the moment?'

Ravi messaged her, finally. During all these happy hours, Meenakshi thought about what Ravi must be thinking at the moment. Maybe not the best time to think about a cheating ex-boyfriend, but his face had remained stuck in her mind ever since he had left Kanpur. She had heard about his struggles in Mumbai and couldn't help feeling some satisfaction.

'Yes, it was a fantastic evening.' She wanted to write a lot else but this was not the time.

'Wow! I'm proud of you, Meenakshi!'

'Are you, now?'

'Come on, darling! I still think you are the most beautiful woman in the world. Now that your face will be everywhere in the city, can I get a picture just for myself only?'

Meenakshi's face flushed, but this time it was probably not just fever. She remembered how Ravi used to love it when she blushed.

She decided to send him a selfie. He should see the skyline of the city behind her. She turned on the front camera and held it in front of her face. She shrieked and the phone fell from her hand.

Whose hand was that? She picked up the phone with shaking hands and held up the front camera. A thin ashen black hand was holding her face. She tried to shake it off her face. When she tried to touch it, the hand scattered like a black smoke. Then it formed the shape of the hand and covered her face again. Her heart beating wildly, she started running from the roof and almost tripped on the staircase. She frantically pushed the button in the elevator for her apartment. As soon as she entered, she ran to the basin to splash water on her face and her whole head. The cold splash of water eased the burning sensation. She felt better and took the towel beside the mirror to dry off. She looked at the mirror and froze. She had no face any more. Instead, the nostrils and two popping eyes were the only features left where her face used to be.

Characteristics of the munchowa
- Attacks late at night.
- Steals a person's face.
- Doesn't kill.
- A ghost found in Kanpur.

52

MUNI PEI

Muni is a ghost that can either be good or bad. It is worshipped in some cultures and feared by others. In some texts—the Rigveda or 'Mariamman Thalattu', a lullaby dedicated to Goddess Mariamman along with references to various deities—muniyadis or muniandis are called guardian angels that protect people from evil and diseases. They become muni either at birth, or, in most cases, when a highly spiritual rishi, king or a learned person dies, and their spirit ascends to muni status. The munis are worshipped alongside their gods and are associated with Lord Shiva or Mahadev and his other half, Shakti.

Texts like 'Kandar Sashti Kavasam'[*] have brought the evil muni spirits to the fore. These creatures are described as having a tail, sharp teeth, and a fierce appearance with a thick moustache. They eat people, babies, have the power of black magic, emit fire from

---

[*]A Hindu devotional song composed during the nineteenth century in Tamil by Devaraya Swamigal, a devotee of Lord Muruga.

their mouths and, sometimes, their powers are equated with that of a brahmarakshasa (see chapter 9).

Some sources like the gurukkals in Malayasia and Singapore say that the sapta munis, or the seven munis, came out of the mouth of Lord Shiva to stop King Daksha from completing his yagna (a sacrifice to the god of fire, Agni). Other texts like the *Vayu Purana* have clarified that the muniyadis or munis had no connection to Daksha's yagna.

Very powerful supernatural spirits, the veeranas, are often counted among the munis. For instance, Madurai veeran is worshipped in temples so that the people of the village are not harmed by diseases and plagues.

Trees are counted as paths or gateways for the munis to travel between the mortal, heavenly, and hellish dimensions. Sometimes, they choose to stay inside trees. Banyan, palmyra, and the sacred fig tree are worshipped as the symbols of munis. Apart from trees, stones and statues are also symbolic of these guardian spirits and are worshipped to keep them satisfied.

Characteristics of the muni pei
- Can be good or evil.
- A supernatural spirit.
- Worshipped widely in Tamil culture.

53

MUNISH

The munish is considered an angel in Bengali folklore. The munish is believed to walk around the yard of the house of the family it's protecting. It does so at night, wearing white clothing and a kharam, or wooden sandals. Some say that they appear in the dreams that the family members have. When contented, it appears in their dreams and gives reassurances of well-being. If the munish is unhappy, it can cause nightmares and insomnia among the infants and the young ones in the family.

Barring some exceptions, worshipping a munish is considered a good omen.

They are a kind of undead spirit, living in a transitional phase between life and death. It is believed that an honest, highly religious member of a family can become a munish upon dying in order for them to keep an eye on their family's well-being. The members of the family would worship the spirit to keep it satisfied.

Apart from causing sleep deprivation among infants, the munish has other methods to notify people about its unhappiness.

For example, the munish's footsteps can be heard by the side of a pond. This is a sign of dire displeasure with the family. To assuage the situation, the head of the family must then bring a black magic practitioner to the family and have them assess the demands of the munish by performing certain rituals. Once the munish's demands are made known, the family should follow the shaman's advice and enact the correct rituals. Various kinds of sweetmeats, a potful of milk, and a new piece of dhoti are gifted to the spirit.

The following day, the family members must bathe in that pond and taste the offerings after paying due respect to the munish, and distribute them among the neighbours.

Characteristics of the munish
- Usually a benevolent spirit.
- Watches over families.
- The spirit of a recently departed member of the family.
- Found in Bengal.

54

MUNJYA

In Hinduism, life is considered to have four distinctive phases. The first cycle begins as a student. A child has to go through the rituals of upanayan or the holy thread ceremony, also called munja in Marathi. This has to be carried out when the child's age is an odd number. The child is taught sacred hymns, a strict lifestyle with no luxuries. This phase is called brahmacharya.

The student grows into a learned man, gets married and enters the grihastha phase. He's now a family man. There are sod munja rituals performed as a part of the marriage rituals. They are nearly identical to the upanayana; the former marked the beginning of brahmacharya, the latter marks the end. The family man is a provider and caretaker; he has to look after his wife and children.

When the man grows old, he is expected to move away from society. Leaving all his belongings behind, he should lead a holy life amidst the forest and nature. This phase is vanaprastha, after completing which he is left to pray and wait for a peaceful death. The final phase is called sannyasa.

Not all people are able to complete this phase of life exactly as prescribed. They die prematurely, so to speak. Those who die in the time between the munja and the sod munja rituals—that is, those who never leave the brahmacharya stage, are stuck in the mortal world as a spirit called the munjya.

The munjya resides either in peepul trees or close to wells. They do not harm people. Timid and mischievous, they just scare people who might be walking alone under a peepul tree or by a well in the evening.

The munjya is known to hop around trees, which is explained by the Marathi idiom, 'bara pimpala varcha munjya', meaning, a person who can't rest, but hops from one task to another.

There are two possible explanations for the creation of this ghost in Marathi folklore. The first is that it is meant as a cautionary tale to people to not hesitate to get married and therefore enter the best phase of their lives. The other possible explanation is that peepul trees, huge and leafy, produce vast quantities of carbon dioxide after sunset. If a person stays in their shade for a long period of time, they could suffocate or experience hallucinations, and the munjya was invented to scare them away.

Characteristics of the munjya
- Harmless spirit.
- Resides in peepul trees or near wells at sundown.
- Found in Maharashtra.

55

NALI BA

Before everyone realized what it meant to have multinational business hubs in a city, Bangalore, ahead of the curve, welcomed people from all across the country. It took a while for Amal to convince himself and his family about migrating to this new city, but it paid off. His small yet cosy flat helped him get over homesickness. However, the interfering neighbours, who constantly bombarded him with advice on the importance of marriage, remained his only concern.

Although it was slightly irritating at times when a neighbourhood uncle would visit him after office hours to check if his plumber had come on time, or when the mother of a marriageable girl surprised him with a pot of fish curry prepared by her daughter, Amal nevertheless liked the neighbourly warmth he experienced in the building. Each time the doorbell rang, he'd sigh and give up his favourite TV show since it usually took about an hour to get rid of them. Sometimes their visits overlapped, too. One night, while Mr Chaturvedi was sitting on his couch advising him on his political views, somebody else knocked mildly on the door. Amal reached for the door, but Mr Chaturvedi swiftly blocked his way. He went close to the door and firmly said 'nali ba', which meant 'come tomorrow'.

He advised Amal to never open the door on a knock rather than the bell. Feeling embarrassed about Mr Chaturvedi's rudeness, Amal realized that perhaps the relationship between his neighbours was hostile. Mr Chaturvedi looked uncomfortable when Amal suggested checking who was at the door and left soon after. Amal had a feeling that Mr Chaturvedi knew the person at his door.

The following day, Amal, feeling curious, paid visits to the other neighbours and tried to find out who had visited his flat, but nobody said anything. He even asked one of the families who visited him frequently, who said, looking uncomfortable, that they never knocked at his apartment and rang the bell if necessary. Amal was unable to trace his mystery visitor. Mr Chaturvedi never visited him again. Amal sometimes went to their home where he was still welcomed but Mr Chaturvedi avoided Amal's flat.

One midnight, there was a knock on his door. Amal, hesitating, realized that his neighbour was right. Why should anybody come to his flat at this hour? Unable to suppress his curiosity, he decided to look into the peephole. He saw an eye staring through the peephole from the other side.

Amal reeled back in surprise and decided to not open the door. He whispered 'nali ba' just as Mr Chaturvedi had done. After a few moments, he checked again. The eye was gone.

The next day he visited Mr Chaturvedi, who told him a horrifying tale of an evil spirit that sometimes knocked on doors at night. It had to be told to 'come tomorrow'.

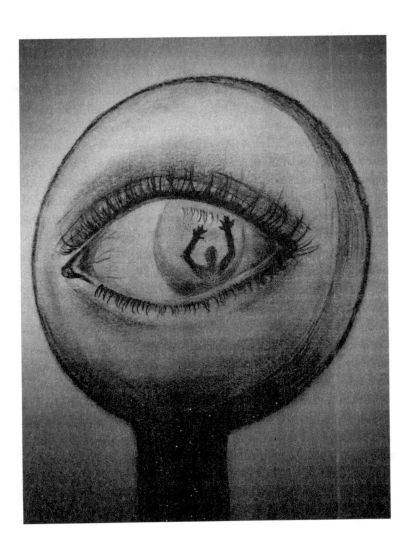

Feeling uneasy, Amal wasn't sure if he believed the story. But nobody knocked on his door again and, gradually, he forgot about the whole thing.

Soon, after a promotion at work, his marriage was fixed. The whole residential complex came together to celebrate his wedding. Amal marvelled at how his soaring career had made him popular. Then, things fell apart. His company was mixed in a money laundering scandal, and Amal's name was connected to it. His image fell apart. The landlord gave him a moving-out notice. All his neighbours melted away. Saddened and desperate, Amal decided to kill himself. As he fastened a rope to the ceiling fan in his flat, he thought bitterly of his neighbours.

Knock, knock, knock. Finally, someone had come to check on him. He opened the door.

There was nobody outside. After checking the corridor, he came back inside. His head felt heavy and drowsy. Looking up to the ceiling, he realized the makeshift noose was swinging slightly. He felt sick. The pain in his chest started building and he felt suffocated. He walked out to get some help and rang the bell of the apartment next door. When the bell did not ring, he knocked on the door.

'Nali ba,' they said.

He froze on the spot. After getting the same response from every door, he came back with trembling knees to find his door ajar, with his motionless body lying at the doorway.

Characteristics of the nali ba

- Knocks on doors at night.
- If their knocks are answered, it causes death.
- Can be seen in Bangalore.

56

NISHIDAAK

'Haradhan!'

The booming voice of Ramkali Tantrik echoed through the courtyard. Haradhan wasn't home. His wife came running to the door with a handful of rice grains for Ramkali.

'You took long! Never make me call twice.'

'Never again, Thakur!' she begged for mercy.

Ramkali left for the next house. For almost a decade, he had lived at the edge of the village as the saviour of these people. Everybody acknowledged him as the godman who protected the village from evil. He'd come to their houses from time to time and demand alms, which the villagers gave as an act of devotion, or sometimes out of sheer fright. Ramkali had warned them to answer on his first call. He never called twice. If they didn't answer the first call he'd leave. If the person was fated to die, he'd call twice and the family would be subsequently struck by a calamity. The villagers had seen the mysterious death of Tinkori's eldest daughter when she didn't respond to the tantrik's call.

Ramkali stopped for a second on the doorstep of Giridas's house. He'd heard they had a newborn in the family last month. But the child had not been brought for sanctification yet! Ramkali got very annoyed at people failing to obey the rules. A few years ago, they had rushed their eldest son to Ramkali for severe stomach pain. He still couldn't hide the smile on his lips when he remembered giving them a pot of sugar syrup disguised as 'divine drops' which cured the boy's jaundice. He learnt all these tricks from his master. He knew some basic tactics to deal with the crises people underwent. Though, once in a while, you have to show some miracles. Curing Giridas's eldest son was one of those significant milestones that kept people intrigued about Ramkali's divine powers.

'Giridas!' Ramkali roared outside their door.

His voice had always triggered awe among the villagers. The family came running, begging mercy for not bringing the child to see him earlier. They blamed the mother, the wife of the younger brother of Giridas, who refused to take her son to be sanctified. She clearly had no respect for rituals and refused to obey the elders, they said.

This triggered a memory at the back of Ramkali's head. He remembered the last time Tinkari's wife refused to come to his hut for the sacrificial rites he performed on the nights of eclipse. All the other women to whom he'd proffered this opportunity had been overwhelmed and had devoted themselves to his will. He was irascible when people dared to refuse the wrath of destiny.

'Nishi might come for you; did you know that, Giridas? You know that Nishi can come down upon you and bring disaster to the family?' Ramkali kept his voice composed.

Before Giridas could answer, the slightly frightened yet bold voice of the young girl rang out from the back of the crowded room.

'Nishi calls the person it wants to harm. I've read about it. Why does the evil come for the women in this village?'

Ramkali couldn't believe his ears. Never in his life had anybody dared to question him. The young girl with bright eyes and curly hair, holding a small child in her arms, looked into his eyes. The room fell silent. They were frightened of the consequences of such audacity in front of a godman.

'Good that you have read about them. Have you read that when Nishi calls a person, only they can hear it? Nobody knew when the final call was made for the poor souls and took them to their destiny. I called someone from the family twice by their name, to make them aware of the upcoming disaster. I can foresee such mishaps.'

The tension in the room lightened. Everybody seemed grateful for the answer and asked for more blessings for the family. The girl didn't say anything more, but she still refused to present the child at Ramkali's feet for blessings. Quietly, she left the room with her child. People were so shocked they didn't even know how to beg for mercy. They offered him a lot of alms but Ramkali refused and left the house.

On his way home, he felt his hands trembling with excitement. He had never wanted a woman so badly. Nobody had invoked such desire in him. He knew what he had to do; just a matter of few days, and he could place the malaise on the family and get what he wanted. He planned on taking it slow, just like in the past. The curly locks on that woman's head could not be a one-time experience.

Once he reached home, he couldn't sit or get changed for hours. He had collected a decent quantity of groceries that day, but he had no interest in sorting them out or starting the evening fire. So instead, he paced through his courtyard in the dark. The big tree at the back of his house cast a long shadow that made the hut even darker. The dense silence of the night was only broken by the footsteps of Ramkali. The tree remained absolutely still, no leaves rustling in the wind. To be precise, there was no wind. Ramkali stopped pacing and waited for any sound in the eerie silence.

'Ramkali…Ramkali….'

Characteristics of the nishidaak

- An evil voice that calls twice at night.
- If answered, its prey is doomed.
- No one who has experienced it has lived to tell the tale.
- Extremely harmful.
- Folk tales advise one should never answer a call at night if it is not repeated three times.
- Mentioned in tales from Bengal.

57

PANDABBA

The best part of having a pond in a village is sitting by it, especially in the evening, when the breeze is blowing. On warm afternoons, the villagers could sit beside the pond to cool down and relax. After a tiring day, they would sit together and discuss life, or play cards. When Hiralal arrived at the village with his wife to visit his in-laws, he spent his time by the side of the pond or loafing around with the villagers.

His life with his wife was mostly peaceful except for one issue. His wife was irritated by his addiction to bidis. She despised the smell and every time Hiralal lit up a smoke to enjoy a puff, she'd complain about the unbearable smell. So, he tried to smoke outside the house at all times. Even during sleepless nights, he would go into the backyard to enjoy a bidi in peace. Before his marriage, he would smoke while finishing his morning ablutions. But due to his wife's complaints about the smell of smoke in the toilet, every day he woke up early to clear up the smoke by the time others used it. On the days he'd sleep a bit longer than usual, he would have to

go to the fields. His in-laws' house was no exception. He would sit with his father-in-law who would complain about how he had to give up smoking due to the tantrums of Hiralal's mother-in-law. He sometimes accompanied Hiralal on his backyard adventures when both of their wives took an afternoon nap.

The pondside was a relief for Hiralal as the villagers would sit together and smoke bidis. But he couldn't help feeling there was something odd about this village. Once, he saw a man walk towards a group of people and ask for a bidi, at which the villagers scuttled away, dragging Hiralal with them. Surprised, Hiralal felt pity for the man. He only asked for a bidi! That poor man must have troubles like him or his father-in-law about smoking at home. Why wouldn't people give him a single puff? The villagers, however, didn't want to answer his questions. Later, his father-in-law told him that the village folklore advised that one should never share a smoke by the pondside. It was the ghost called pandabba who asks for a bidi by the pondside. If you try to share a puff, the ghost will seize your hand, drag you into the pond, and drown you.

He figured this tale was just to discourage people from sharing bidis. He wondered what people of this village, especially the women, had against the smoking of bidis. He should have checked these facts before getting married here. Even his father-in-law agreed with him, while serenely puffing a bidi in the backyard of the house. Unluckily, they were caught by his wife who started shouting immediately to alert her mother as well. Both of them especially scolded Hiralal for dragging the old man into this. He and his father-in-law tried to explain themselves, but neither woman would listen. They seized the pack of bidis along with the money bag. Hiralal protested and tried to explain his point of view, but in vain. After a while, he left the house and went to the pondside.

The area was deserted. Lost in his thoughts, he didn't really pay attention when someone came and sat beside him. It was the same man who was refused a bidi the other day. Hiralal knew this person must have been in a situation like his. He tried to talk to him politely. The man looked surprised. Hiralal asked the man for a bidi.

Surprised, the man got to his feet. Hiralal tried to calm him down, but the more he tried to talk to him, the more frightened the man grew. Then he ran towards the pond and dove into the water. Hiralal followed him in but, to his surprise, there was nobody in the water.

On turning around, he saw a few petrified faces, who had seen the entire incident, staring at him. From that day onwards, Hiralal became known as the famous ghost chaser and, ironically, nobody, not even the shopkeepers, would give him a bidi any more.

Characteristics of the pandabba

- Lives in ponds.
- Asks for a bidi. If a bidi is shared, the ghost seizes the outstretched hand and drowns its victim in the pond.
- Found in the villages of Bihar.

58

PARI

The pari is a spirit of Persian origin. A variant of the fairies from the western world, paris are popular in South Asian countries. There are both good and bad paris. In this context, 'bad' does not indicate being harmful to humans, but rather mischievous. The harmful subspecies of paris are named 'divs' or 'daeva'.

The paris are born in both male and female forms and are believed to be exquisitely beautiful. The Persian concept of paris was adapted into Turkish and Armenian tales of mythology and, as people migrated, stories about them seeped into Islamic cultures and evolved under the religious influence.

Due to their notorious nature, paris are not allowed to enter heaven. Instead, they have to spend a lifetime doing good work or lamenting in order to be purified before they are granted access to heaven. The Persian tales associate these mythological beings mostly with scenarios depicting love, romance, and beauty.

In Persian cosmology, they live in a place called Paristan or Pariestan located in the icy mountains. Young, beautiful, and fair-

skinned females living in the valley around Mount Qaf, especially women with golden hair and light eyes, were also referred to as paris or fairies.

According to some sources, paris are believed to be only females and not males. They punish hunters who disrespect nature. They also abduct children for their social events, thus making the nature of pari–human interactions both psychological and physical.

Characteristics of the pari

- Largely a benevolent spirit.
- Very beautiful and mischievous.
- Associated with romance.
- Of Persian origin but found throughout Asia.

59

PISHACHAS

Of the plethora of monsters and demons to be found in Hindu mythology, pishachas are one of the few to be truly deadly. They speak in a language called Paisachi and have a monstrous appearance, with a dark human-like body, protruding veins, and huge, fierce, red eyes.

Unlike many other neighbourhood ghosts, pishachas are not born out of the souls of dead people, but have supernatural origins. They dwell around crematoriums; their companions are bhootas and vetalas. Pishachas can possess humans, take shapes at will, and disappear from human sight when they want to.

There are religious ceremonies devised to free a human body that has been possessed by a pishacha. They possess the power to turn people insane, control their minds, which may render the human unconscious from time to time.

The pishachas can be killed by the swing of a blessed or enchanted sword. But, even after being killed, their souls will haunt the spot where they were buried or cremated until appropriate religious ceremonies are performed to rid the place of their evil.

In Hindu mythology, pishachas are described as the offspring of the sage Kashyapa and Krodha (anger) or Krodhavasa (one of the daughters of Daksha, a Hindu deity).

Pishachas have journeyed into the folklore of the Hindu–Buddhist tradition in Thailand and are depicted in several Buddhist temples.

Characteristics of the pishachas

- Monstrous spirit.
- Encounter with it is usually fatal.
- Supernatural origin.
- Found throughout India and Southeast Asia.

60

POTACHUNNI

To escape the scorching heat in the summer afternoons, Rumi would run off to one of the rooms that was always cooler than the rest of the house, to spend time with Rani. Since she and Ashoke had moved to this small town, Rumi had been managing everything on her own. Ashoke was delighted to be able to cheaply rent this huge bungalow. When Rumi could no longer manage all the household chores, they hired Rani.

From the beginning, Rumi had liked the girl for her cheerfulness and simplicity. Maybe it was slightly odd to spend time with their maid but being away from her friends immediately after marriage, Rumi needed a friend. Rani was a good listener, always expressing surprise at the correct points. She was also empathetic when Ashoke was unfair. Soon, Rumi found herself confiding all her troubles to her maid, including her marital woes. Rani would make sympathies, including how she could control her husband by withholding sex. As the days went by, Rumi found the stratagems suggested by the maid to be very effective especially when it came to her love life. She and her husband grew closer, not least in the bedroom. She would somehow wonder how Rani came up with all her tricks and plays—it wasn't as though she was married or had many romantic relationships. She was not attractive, had dark skin, and a perpetually runny nose; it was hard to see a man being attracted to her. On occasion, she would feel guilty about listening to Rani's suggestions, wouldn't the other woman envy the stimulating relationship she shared with her husband—especially in bed!

Sometimes she fancied Rani was jealous of her relationship with her husband. At other times, she would feel aroused thinking of Rani fantasizing about her sexual and romantic life with her husband. On occasion, she would imagine Rani peeping through the keyhole when she and Ashoke had sex.

One night, the feeling that she was being watched when she was having sex was so vivid, she even fancied she could *see* a woman with a runny nose peeping into her room. She was so shaken that she pushed Ashoke away. He tried to calm her down but Rumi continued to be agitated. She waited until morning to confront Rani.

Rani admitted that she had been trying to spy on them, citing her burning curiosity. Rumi couldn't bring herself to explain to Ashoke why Rani was curious. This repeated a couple more times. Rumi even started finding her things in Rani's room sometimes. Like her sari or undergarments from the night before, or even her cosmetics. Out of patience, when she caught Rani wearing her sankha bangle[*] that she safely kept in her locker, she told Ashoke

---

[*]A bangle made of seashells worn by a married woman in Bengali culture.

the details of Rani's curiosity. Carefully skipping the part where she had sought her help, she told him how Rani might be desperate to have a life like them which was causing all the issues. Ashoke brushed the matter aside.

Rumi told Rani that she'd have to leave in a few days, to which the latter just smiled and agreed. Rumi started spending more time out of the house with her husband. The nights weren't as fun as they used to be, but she assumed they would go back to normal once that woman left the house. Imagining how she would throw Rani out of the house and shut the door on her face gave her relief. That night, Rumi slept soundly.

She woke up with a cold and a heavy head. The dark room gave her chills and she realized she was not in her room. As she sat up with a jolt, something slimy rolled down her nose. Wiping it with the back of her hand, she shuddered at the thick phlegm stuck on her hand. Then she realized that she was wearing the sankha bangle on her hands. She couldn't remember wearing them last night. She looked around. It was Rani's room. Her heart racing wildly, she quickly walked towards the main bedroom. The door was ajar. Rani was asleep on her bed holding Ashoke.

Characteristics of the potachunni
- A type of shankhchunni.
- Always has phlegm running from its nose.
- When a married woman dies with unfulfilled desires, she turns into this ghost.
- Kills people.
- Found in Bengal.

61

PRAPTI

First: How long did it take you?

Second: Almost an hour. But this one won't take that long.

First: Good for him. He looks scared, though. Do you think he can still get away?

Second: No way. Look how he has tied his hands behind his back. He knew he could lose his nerves in the end, so be prepared for that eventuality.

First: Must be her. She knew this one always lacked courage. Never figured out how she tolerated this guy.

Second: The question is not how, but why? Don't get offended but you never really could satisfy her needs, could you? She spent many sleepless nights looking at the ceiling, feeling lonely, while you were chasing after promotions at work. Never took her loneliness seriously.

First: And you still believe that? I'm sure if she was looking at the ceiling then someone must have been doing his job properly.... Sometimes that was you!

Second: Well, at least I tried to be by her side....

First: And where is she now? Did you believe that she would be by your side? Just like this idiot who still thinks she will stand in this room with him after it's all over....

Second: Maybe we should leave now and wait for him to get over the initial heartbreak. Do you remember how the gym instructor panicked when he saw us?

First: It was his old habit of getting scared at the sight of the husband. Did you call him today?

Second: Yes, he still believes she will come looking for him.

First: He came to be useful though. Gave us the information about this man. Why didn't you know about this one? You were so proud of knowing all about your childhood friend!

Second: I told you about the gym guy. Don't blame me, why couldn't you figure it out? You were her husband for almost five years and the only one you could suspect was a childhood friend.

First: I was right though! I doubted her many times. But who in their right mind would suspect a different man each time he felt like his wife is cheating on him?

Third: Have you seen her?

First: Ah! The muscleman. Welcome onboard.

Second: No, she must have left before we arrived.

First: Don't look sad! We'll get more chances.

Third: Please don't say that. This is already a mess.

First: Feeling embarrassed, are you? Girls were ready to give up their lives for you. How does it feel now?

Second: Do you know of anybody else? Did she tell you anything else about herself?

Third: We never really talked much....

First: Of course, why would you waste time talking!

Third: ...she used to come to the gym with this guy sometimes and he'd wait in the reception lounge for hours. Then I began to have an inkling of what was going on.

First: Mr Muscles, you must be really stupid if it took you so long to realize this woman was deadly, and not to be trusted.

Second: Oh, please, you are the one with the most myopic vision. If you had the barest of observation skills, you could have noticed the distance building up between you two.

First: And what did you do? You could see right through her heart. Why did she need more people even after having you at her disposal? Because some people just keep searching without realizing what they are looking for. You are the poet; you know poetry glorified these people as 'the seekers'. But in reality, they are just a bunch of confused people who gradually become harmful for everybody around them.

Second: Then why did you do it? If you knew she was never
             going to be by your side, no matter what she says, why
             did you fall for her words again? When she committed
             suicide, you were shattered. Then she came along and
             manipulated you like anybody else here....

First: You are the analytical man dealing with psychology,
             look at all her victims—this guy, a man with physical
             strength and confidence, and this one, still struggling
             to catch his last breath, was a journalist. She had the
             ability to sound like she was repentant even after
             committing hideous activities. She held the bottle of
             sleeping pills right in front of me and asked me to
             give her one last chance to be with her. How could
             I deny her?

Second: We tried to learn to swim in that river when we were
             children and failed. She knew I never learnt to swim.
             Before I jumped in, she said we'd start right there,
             from our very first failure.

Third: Okay I get it, all of us failed in many ways. Do you
             know if there will be a fifth and if there is any chance,
             we can get hold of her before the tragedy takes place?

Fourth: She already killed the fifth. I helped her. It was
             her cousin. I told him I'll expose his incestuous
             relationship and he couldn't handle that. I'm glad I
             didn't have to watch him slit his hand.

Characteristics of the prapti

- Female ghost.
- Attacks everyone she has even been in a relationship with.
- Kills by making them commit suicide.
- When a confused woman with multiple relationships in her life commits suicide, she becomes this ghost.
- Found in West Bengal.

62

PRETA

The word preta comes from the Sanskrit language. In the cultural tales of India, Sri Lanka, China, Japan, Korea, Vietnam, Tibet, Thailand, Cambodia, Laos, and Myanmar, across religions including Hinduism, Buddhism, and Taoism, the preta finds mention. Even in Chinese culture there is a mention of a 'hungry ghost' that resembles the image of the preta. It is believed that these supernatural beings had originated in Indian religions before they were adopted by the Buddhists and tales of the pretas spread across Asia alongside the spread of Buddhism. The pretas are believed to be the ghosts suffering from an unquenchable thirst and insatiable hunger.

From as early as 300 BC, in the scriptures like the *Petavatthu* from the oldest Buddhist schools, called Theravada, they were simply described as ghosts, but later evolved into beings who arose in the transient state between death and rebirth. In many Asian cultures it is believed that everyone passes through a cycle of karmic reincarnation. When a person dies, if the family does not perform the correct rituals to free his soul and guide him to his next life within a year of his death, his soul would be trapped as a preta for the rest of eternity.

People who, in their lifetimes, are liars, corrupt, tricky, envious, or greedy are believed to be pretas after their death. They have disturbing visions and, due to their karma, they have an unsatiable hunger. Pretas cannot be seen by humans under normal conditions, but sometimes, they can be seen as mummified version of the human form with narrow arms and legs, long necks, and a sunken belly. In some cultures, they are shown to be taking form amidst balls of smoke or fire, in other places, they are depicted as licking spilled water from temples. They dwell in wastelands and since they find it very difficult to forage for food, they are constantly hungry. The sufferings of pretas are often compared with the dwellers in hell, only that the pretas can move around in the world while denizens of hell cannot.

In some Hindu scriptures, they are considered atmas bound for a rebirth. The transient period of the soul is pure and every time, except in the last form of physical birth, they are considered to be comparable to the gods. Rice balls are offered by the family of the deceased to the preta to guide them into their next lives.

In Buddhist cultures, the preta is considered as one of the

five forms of existence. In Japan, where they are called gaki, celebrations are held wherein offerings are made to free them from their torment. In Sri Lankan culture, humans with excess of greed are believed to be reincarnated as pretas.

The pretas are pitied as poor supernatural creatures and, in certain Buddhist monasteries, the monks offer them food, money, flowers, etc., before meals. Their importance is celebrated in Tibetan Buddhist traditions as well as the Chinese Taoist tradition, where paper idols and models of symbols of materialism are burnt for the spirits.

Most pretas are considered merely 'irritating', except for when they are thirsting for blood. They can change their faces, turn invisible and, using the means of magic and illusions to frighten humans, can prevent them from achieving their goals.

Characteristics of the preta
- A supernatural being to be found in many Asian cultures.
- Also called hungry ghosts.
- Is believed to come into being in the world between a person's death and rebirth if the person was evil or a proper funeral ceremony was not conducted.
- Mostly harmless.

63

PUTANA

Putana was a demoness who was sent by Kansa, Lord Krishna's uncle, in order to slay his nephew. The daughter of the asura king Bali in her previous life, her name was Ratnamala. She had once breastfed Vamana, another avatar of Vishnu. For that, Lord Vishnu had blessed Ratnamala. In her life as a demoness, Putana was unaware of that blessing.

She descended upon Krishna's hometown in the form of a beautiful young woman. Krishna's foster-mother, Yashoda, who mistook Putana for one of the gopis, allowed her to take young Krishna on her lap and breastfeed him. Krishna, however, knew she wanted to kill him and that her breasts were smeared with poison. Several versions of this story exist. Some of them describe the breast milk itself as poisonous while others suggest Yashoda did not hand over the child. Rather, Putana arrived in the darkness of the night and stole the child.

Suckling on the milk, Krishna then proceeded to kill her by squeezing her breasts, taking her milk and her life out of her body.

In doing so, he also freed her body of all sins, and she is considered as another foster-mother of the lord and is believed to have attained the same heaven as Yashoda did.

In some sources, it is said that Krishna only killed Putana's mortal body, freeing her soul. Putana is depicted as a rakshasi who protected children, as well as a priestess or alternatively a yogini. In an unnamed medical text, Putana is the name of one of Ravana's sixteen sisters who ate the flesh of infants.

Putana is believed to symbolize many childhood diseases which may result in fatality. Several ancient Indian texts recommend worshipping Putana to protect children from various diseases. Similarly, another demon was named jwara (fever) whom Lord Krishna fought with later.

Characteristics of the putana

- A demoness, and the daughter of the asura king Bali.
- Tried to kill Lord Krishna but was killed by him.
- Is dangerous to infants.

64

PUWALI

'So, you just keep practising?'

'Yes, every day!'

'All types of sweets that are available in town?'

'All types.'

Afreen took quick notes in her notepad. This story was turning out to be a lot more interesting than she thought. Initially, she was sceptical about taking up this food-blogging assignment for the magazine. But each time she visited a new place on her hunt for traditional Indian foods, she found that each Indian heritage dish had a unique history. In Assam, when she visited a village that was famous for its unique sweets, Afreen met a fascinating old lady. The local sweet makers called her the mother of the recipes of some famous delicacies. Even though this was not the focus of her story, Afreen couldn't help spending a lot of time with the lady talking about her life. Living in the huge, old house with couple of servants who had been loyal to her for years, she spent all her days making every kind of famous sweet that had its origin in the village.

She was generous and offered some of her exquisite preparations to Afreen. She made the sweets for Afreen. However, there was something off about the feast of sweets she was organizing. She made only one of every kind, with the exception of a sample of sweets of which she made two portions. When she had finished making all the sweets, she arranged them on a tray, and asked Afreen to partake of the feast. There was way more than she could eat even if she were to exert herself, so she asked the old lady what would become of the rest.

'Where do they go, all these sweets? You can't possibly eat them all!'

'Nowhere!'

Afreen felt depressed on hearing the fate of these sumptuous desserts. It made her even more curious about this old lady. She kept coming back every day to hear more of her stories—about the time when she got married to the richest and most skilled confectioner of the city, or when her son went to the UK and never returned, or when her husband died and left all the recipes to her, etc. Afreen could sense the loneliness in her voice. All this wasted effort could be her desire to make something for her dear ones. Yet there was no regret towards this wasted labour; rather she sounded like this was the best job that she could do at the moment.

Perhaps being a journalist had made her very curious, but Afreen couldn't take her mind off the enigmatic lady and her peculiar sweet-making routine. Where did all the sweets go? She observed the house from the nearest vantage point. Each night she saw the lady through the kitchen window, making sweets and arranging them on trays. Then leaving all the trays beside the window, she would turn off the kitchen lights. One night, Afreen decided to linger a little longer in case she returned. But the old lady did not come back. Frustrated, she waited until midnight. Just when she had completely lost hope, she heard a light footstep behind her. Startled, she turned and found the old lady walking towards her.

The lady looked into her eyes for a while, then indicated that she should follow without saying a word. Once they were inside the house, she went to a first-floor window. From there, she pointed to the kitchen window where was visible in the moonlight, a small, fat, white figure of a boy taking the sweets through the window.

Characteristics of the puwali

- A child ghost.
- Steals sweets from the kitchen.
- A free spirit.
- Completely harmless.
- Found in Assam.

65

PYACHAPECHI

'There! Do you see it now?'

'No, I'm afraid not. Pravin, please forget about the bird.'

'But I'm telling you that I am going to follow it.'

Bimal looked about anxiously. This was the third time he had lost sight of Pravin. They were approaching a bend in the rough track they were on, and Pravin, who was ahead of him, disappeared around the bend. Thick forests hemmed in the path on all sides. The batteries in his torch were running out of juice and the light from it was growing dimmer, all when he was supposed to keep a strict eye on him. What excuse would he give this time to Pravin's wife? He knew it could make her suspicious if he said that her husband just vanished from his sight right after entering the forest.

She had asked Bimal to watch over Pravin on their way back from the station. It was usually a fifteen-minute walk from the station through the forest but Pravin kept taking longer and longer to make his way home with every passing day. According to his wife, he was initially late by thirty minutes, which increased gradually. For the past few days, he was getting late for more than an hour. To allay her concerns, his wife asked Pravin's close friend and co-passenger, Bimal, to watch him on his way back. However, he had secretly told Bimal that an owl had followed him on his way home. Bimal couldn't explain this weird story to Pravin's wife. He agreed to give him company on the way home but this was the third time he had lost track of Pravin within a few moments of entering the forest.

Growing desperate, he looked around. The deeper he went into the forest, the colder it got. A slight chill ran up his spine. Even though it sounded mad he couldn't help checking the trees behind him every now and then. After a while he gave up looking for Pravin and walked out of the forest as fast as he could. He waited at the tea shop close to Pravin's house and spotted him walking in after another hour. Before he could say anything, Pravin came straight to him.

'Where were you?' Bimal asked.

'What do you mean? We were together.'

'Yes, but you left after a while. Where did you go?'

'You must have lost your way! I followed the owl; it knows the way.'

'Tell me, Pravin, does the bird follow you? Or do you follow the bird?'

Looking uncomfortable, Pravin said he'd be more careful.

The following day, Pravin never reached home. His wife lost her mind and cursed Bimal for being a useless friend. Bimal cursed himself, too, for abandoning his friend. Despite an official complaint and a police search, Pravin was nowhere to be found.

Every day, on his way back from the station, Bimal would feel a tingle run up his spine while walking through the forest. There was something clearly wrong with this place and he walked as fast as he could.

'What took you so long?' his wife asked him.

'What do you mean? I walked even faster my usual!'

'Don't lie to me. You were late by almost twenty minutes yesterday. Today it's almost half an hour. Where did you go?'

'Nowhere, I followed the owl. It knows the way.'

Characteristics of the pyachapechi

- An owl ghost that leads travellers astray.
- When they lose the way, it kills them.
- Can be seen in Bengal.

66

RAKSHASA

Rakshasas play an important role in Indian myths, classics, and in folklore. They are the infamous demigods from Hindu mythology. They are similar to asuras who take human form often and eat humans. According to the Puranic stories, they emerged from the breath of Brahma when he was asleep, at the end of the Satya Yuga. These blood-lusting creatures began devouring Brahma himself. When Vishnu heard the god's cry for help, he banished all these creatures to earth. Their name came from Brahma's cry for help, 'rakshama' which means, 'protect me'. In the Rigveda, they are categorized as mythological supernatural beings who consume raw flesh. In other languages like Indonesian and Malay, the word rakshasa means giant or gigantic, monstrous. In Bengali, the word translates to someone who eats a lot without needing to stop.

Rakshasas are big, frightening, and ugly; they have two big fangs emerging from the top of the mouth and long claws. They can fly, become invisible, and through the magic of illusion, take the shape of any creature. They were great warriors as well. These creatures were mentioned as both good and evil in the Ramayana as well as the Mahabharata. They fought as soldiers under some warlords and did a great amount of damage to enemy soldiers on the battlefield.

In the Ramayana, the people of Lanka were described as rakshasas. They served their king Ravana and fought against the army of Rama. Ravana's brother Kumbhakarna had a frightening appearance, a huge size, and enormous appetite for food, and he fought against the Vanara army of Rama. In contrast, Ravana's brother, Vibhishana was a good rakshasa and he helped Ram in winning the battle.

In the Mahabharata, Hidimba was a cannibal rakshasa, and he was killed by Bhima. Hidimba's sister Hidimbi, a rakshasi, or a female rakshasa, warned the Pandavas before her brother could attack. Bhima later married Hidimbi and their son Ghatotkacha, though a son of human and rakshasi, was born a rakshasa. Ghatotkacha fought in the battle of Kurukshetra and with the help of his magical abilities, caused major damage to the Kaurava army until he was killed by Karna's divine weapon named Shakti.

Apart from Hindu literature, rakshasas are also to be found in Buddhist, Jain, and other folklore. Some rakshasas were mentioned to be harassing Buddha. One of them questioned Buddha's divine knowledge for a prolonged period. Later, being convinced by Buddha's holiness, he chose to be a follower of the religion.

In Jainism, the concept of rakshasa widely varies from that of Hindu and Buddhist concepts. Here, they are considered to be the group of people belonging to a civilized vegetarian kingdom. Their race was 'vidyadhara', meaning 'full of knowledge' and they were devotees of Tirthankara.

Rakshasas are believed to be living among us, although they are invisible to the human eye. They are sometimes harmful, sometimes helpful in building and maintaining peace and sanity.

Characteristics of the rakshasa

- A race of supernatural beings believed to have originated in the breath of Brahma.
- Can be good or evil, but they are usually the latter.
- Ferocious and monstrous in appearance.
- Found in many Asian cultures.

67

REECH

It is possible, on close study, to find similarities between urban culture and tribal belief, especially when it comes to depicting evil. The dark forces that are depicted usually spring from the darkest desires of society, whether they are to be found in cities or deep in the forests. The demon called reech has its origin in these dark desires that I am referring to.

In the forests of Madhya Pradesh, tribes claim that a demon steals their women from their village and abuses them physically. Their goal is to make babies which will perpetuate their kind. What happens to the women after being sexually exploited is not clear. There is no physical description of the reech, since none of the women who have encountered them have lived to tell the tale. A wild, savage appearance is all that has been specified about this demon.

Some of the villages, however, believe that the reech can be tamed if their need to forcibly abduct women is dealt with. So, they make a tribute to them by offering a woman once in a while.

Sometimes even some chickens or ducks are offered in lieu of human sacrifice.

In one of the villages, I discovered a tale of a girl who had started jettisoning tribal rituals as she had outgrown the conservative beliefs of the village. Her parents being somewhat anti-establishment, didn't really bother listening to the threats from the regressive old guard of the village who were threatened by their daughter's attitude. When she started attending schools, they knew it wouldn't be long before she told them she wanted to leave the village and try her fortune in the wider world. Right before the day she was about to leave the village, she mysteriously disappeared. Her parents spent months looking for her. Later someone informed them that she had been seen somewhere in the forest, pregnant and struggling for life. Upon hearing this, the local authorities speculated this as an evidence of the presence of a reech. To pacify the demon, the village elders approached the mother of the abducted girl and tried to prevail upon her to sacrifice herself to the demon so it wouldn't prey upon the rest of them. The father tried to reason with the rest of village by offering the chickens to become the tribute instead, but everyone was so scared they didn't listen to him. Rather they tried to console him with the assurance that all of his past sins of going against the society would be forgiven by this act. To his astonishment, his wife agreed to offer herself to the demon. She told him that if there was indeed a reech, she knew how to take down its power.

The next morning, they escaped from the village through the back door of their hut. The wife still held in her hand the iron rod, sticky with blood, that she had hidden inside her clothes before her encounter with the monster. When it attacked her, she had driven the rod straight into one of its eyes, where its power resided, killing it. There was no further trouble in the village after her act of blinding courage.

Characteristics of the reech

- A monster that preys on women, sexually violating them and killing them.
- Its power resides in its eyes.
- Encounters with it can be fatal.
- Found in the tribal belt, especially in Madhya Pradesh.

68

RUNIA

Evening comes all of a sudden in the mountains, rolling from one range to another. Suraiya witnessed the nearest range gradually melt into the darkness. In the distance, she could hear the church bells ringing as the last light faded. The houses on the mountain looked like a swarm of fireflies as they start turning on the evening lights. Suraiya checked her wristwatch again. Mohan would be here any time now. Her heart was pumping faster than usual. She knew her parents would be devastated for a while. She closed her eyes and swore once again that she'd go back home within a few days and prove them wrong about Mohan. He might appear unreliable, but he did keep his promise and had married Suraiya this morning. In spite of the freezing cold and anxiety she was feeling, she couldn't help but smile thinking about the happy face of her newly married husband. How could she deny him their first night together! Nervously, she checked her wristwatch again.

A few rocks rolled down to her feet. It could be a mild

earthquake, which was not unusual in these mountains. She felt her heartbeat increasing with every passing second. She was used to the cold weather, yet she was shivering as she waited for Mohan to join her on the way to the homestay he had booked for the night. A few smaller rocks rolled down behind her. As she turned around, her heart skipped a beat. Mohan was walking down the stairs out into the surface behind her.

She smiled at him. He looked slightly agitated. Suraiya was surprised to see him alone. He was supposed to come with two of his friends to celebrate the evening.

'They are not coming. They don't approve of our marriage either, and tried to stop me as well. I had to follow an alternative route.' Mohan sounded annoyed.

Suraiya was heartbroken. Rajat and Suri were the only two people on their side. She silently started walking behind Mohan towards the homestay that wasn't very far from here. Mohan was probably feeling worse, she thought. He didn't even hold her hand and walked a few steps ahead of her. The happy man from this morning was no longer visible.

The homestay was owned by an old couple. Far from the chaos of the city, this place was ideal for a romantic getaway. Mohan had booked a room earlier, so they didn't have any problem checking in. The old couple had even placed a few flowers in the bedroom to welcome the newlyweds. Suraiya felt her heartbeat rising again in anticipation of the night ahead. She looked at Mohan who was looking out of the window. He turned around and looked at Suraiya standing awkwardly in the middle of the room.

'What are you waiting for? Take your clothes off!' he said gruffly and abruptly to her utter shock.

Perhaps he, too, was nervous about their first night together. She wondered what she could do to ease the tension in the room. She tried to start a conversation. As she began talking, Mohan moved towards her and hugged her. This was not the first time Mohan had taken her in his arms but this time it felt different. Suraiya tried to calm herself down. But giving in to him felt extremely uneasy. When he started forcing himself on her, she broke off from his embrace and walked out of the room.

She walked towards the small garden in front of the house. There were many rocks scattered everywhere. As she perched on one of them, tears rolled down her eyes. Perhaps her parents were right about Mohan. Just then she heard footsteps. It was the old lady who owned this place. She looked around the garden.

'Where did all of these rocks come from?' She sounded very surprised. 'Oi, girl, what are you doing here alone with the rocks? Go to your room!'

Suraiya felt embarrassed. Perhaps she had overreacted. As she was walking past the front door, a motorbike stopped at the gate across the garden. Rajat and Suri came down from the bike and walk towards her. She tried to be cold to them, but they looked devastated.

'Sorry, Suraiya, we couldn't do anything. There was no warning of the avalanche and he was right there, in front of our eyes on the bike....'

Rajat broke into tears as Suri tried to calm him down.

Suraiya stood rooted to the spot. What were they talking about? She had just seen Mohan a few minutes ago in their room, acting strangely. The old lady, who was standing close, heard the conversation and dragged Suraiya to her room.

The room was empty with only some rocks scattered on the floor. The old lady stared at the rocks, transfixed.

'Did you get married today?' She sounded utterly frightened and looked at her. 'Go back to your home, girl, you are in grave danger.'

Characteristics of the runia

- Male ghost.
- Attacks brides if left alone on their wedding night and tries to sexually abuse them.
- Kills victims by causing avalanches.
- Can be seen in some parts of the Himalaya.

69

SAKINI

Dakini, hakini, kakini, lakini, rakini, and sakini are six sources of female shakti or energies of the tantric branches of worship.

The sakini's roots are deeply embedded in Shaiva philosophy or Shaivism. Sakinis are one among the six yoginis from the yogini-chakra. They are also connected to the study of arts or 'kala adhyan', a part of devi-chakra. Some say they originated from the body of Maha Rudra. The sakini has to be worshipped, placed on a petal of a fresh flower, facing west. They are attendants of Durga and Shiva.

The appearance of the sakini is strange: she has the head of an animal from the cat family, a housecat or a lion, eight-arms, and a smoky ash-coloured complexion.

The concept of sakini evolved into various forms like shakhini, sankhini, and eventually shankhchunni in Bengali folklore. The sankhini is said to be born for the sole purpose of drinking blood from demons. During the clash between Goddess Parvati and the demon Andhakasura, every drop of blood spilled from the demon would generate another evil spirit if the blood touched the ground, so the sankhini was created to gulp down every single drop of blood before it touched the ground.

The sakini is also among the thirty-two yakshinis or yakshis, female yakshas, and she is the guardian spirit responsible for providing people with their clothing, food, and money. She can foresee the future and rarely participates in sexual acts.

In Bengali literature, shankhchunni originates from the sankhini. These types of female ghosts are the trapped spirits of women who die of unnatural causes without having their earthly desires fulfilled or before getting married. The ghost wears a sankha, bangle made of conch shells.

They would wear either gamchha or a red and white-coloured sari. Dark-complexioned with protruding eyes, black tongue, stick-like limbs, saggy breasts, and either a pot belly or a cavity in the place of belly, they can possess humans, drink blood, and drive people insane.

Although none of original sources presuppose evil qualities for the sankhinis, different folklores and traditions ranging from India to Malaysia have attributed them with various forms of evil powers and desires.

Characteristics of the sakini

- A female ghost.
- Has a head of a cat or a lion.
- Is the ghost of women who have died before their time or before marriage.
- Sometimes benevolent, sometimes evil.
- Found in Bengal.

70

SAMANDHA

Many kinds of spirits live among us, invisible to the naked eye. Some of them cause trouble, others are benevolent. Most of them are brought into being when the natural order of things is disrupted. The samandha is a spirit that makes an appearance when someone dies without an heir or if their heir does not perform the correct funeral rituals that enable the spirit of the deceased to leave the world in the prescribed manner.

Without the correct rituals, the spirit gets stuck in the middle of life and death. It can neither reach its final destination for judgement to be passed on its future journey, nor can it live its life on earth. The samandha seeks revenge for not being given due respect during funeral rites. It also seeks a way out of this world. When there is an heir and they fail to properly guide the spirit to the next life, the spirit comes back and makes their lives harder. The samandha could meddle with one's education, cause an unwanted delay in their marriage, and cause hindrances in their career paths.

It does not cause physical harm, nor diseases; it just makes others suffer the same way it has by having to remain on earth.

When astrologers and middlemen attempt to communicate with the samandhas to ask what has upset the spirit, they would often answer the questions. Once the family pays the due respect, performs the rituals, the middleman would summon the samandha again. If the samandha is satisfied, it would let them know.

A satisfied samandha is a good samandha. It would bring peace and sanity in the family, bring success, accelerate careers, and prevent delays in the marriages of family members.

Characteristics of the samandha
- A fairly harmless spirit.
- Rises when proper funeral rites are not performed.

71

SHANKHCHUNNI

Giribala had always been certain of her life choices. Even when something disastrous happened, such as the death of her daughter-in-law, Churni, she would put it down to an unfortunate turn of events, and not to anything she might have done. When Churni, a frail, dark girl had complained about excessive, prolonged menstrual bleeding, Giribala blamed it on her riotous past, although she had no evidence of this. Her son, Rajeev, seemed happy enough with his new bride and would spend hours closeted with her in their room; Giribala expected a grandchild soon enough, but it was not to be. Churni seemed to grow weaker and more exhausted with every passing day—not that this stopped her husband or mother-in-law demanding she satisfy their every desire. When she bled to death, both of them blamed Churni for being unsuited to marriage and the duties of a daughter-in-law.

When Ranjana joined the family as a healthy new bride, Giribala was hopeful her son would be happier. But when she found her son walking mournfully in the garden at dawn after the first night, she was worried. After that she would frequently run into him walking around the house with a hopeless look on his face. Most mornings he would walk in the garden with a gloomy expression. Ranjana seemed useless in other ways as well. Every other day she'd break her sankha, or conch shell bangle, while drawing out water from the well in the garden. After breaking almost a dozen pairs, Giribala forbade her from wearing the sankha. Yet, the next evening, when Giribala saw her drawing water from the well again with a white sankha shining brightly on her hand in the moonlight, she went straight to her son. Rajeev stayed silent. When Ranjana walked in, there was no sankha on her hand. She swore that she had not worn the sankha again.

Giribala waited for the chance to prove herself right. Soon enough, she spotted her from the window of her room hiding under the pallu of her sari with a sankha on her hand. Even though it was late at night, she was sitting on the edge of the well. Now she understood why her son wasn't happy with this woman. How dare she leave his side at this time of the night! She came down the stairs, furious. She walked straight to their room and pushed the door open. To her surprise Ranjana was deep asleep, and Rajeev was nowhere to be seen. The poor boy must be sick of such an insensitive wife who sat on the edge of the well in the middle of the night!

However, Giribala wasn't someone who gave up easily. The next night, after both of them went inside their room, she locked the door silently from outside. Feeling uneasy, she kept looking from her window. Right after midnight, she saw her again. Sitting on the edge of the well. She lifted her head slightly from under her sari pallu to look at Giribala's window. Suddenly, she was very afraid. Something was wrong with the dark thin figure with a glistening sankha on her hand. The figure bore no resemblance to the healthy woman locked in the room downstairs.

A loud bang came from downstairs. Startled, Giribala ran downstairs. She heard Rajeev shouting from inside his room and banging on the door madly. When she opened the door with shaking hands, he rushed past her without a second glance and ran out of the house through the back door. He didn't even bother looking at his mother. Ranjana was sitting on her bed, looking clueless and drowsy, clearly awakened by the noise. Giribala went straight to her.

'What's wrong with you? Why can't he be with you at night? Why don't you let him touch you?' Giribala couldn't control her anger.

'He does not want to have sex. He hates being touched! He said you knew this all along and never want me to go looking for him at night.' Ranjana said, her voice shaky.

Giribala lost her temper. She was sure this woman was making things up. The face under the veil that she could see in her mind's eye, disappointment, and resentment, she pulled Ranjana out of her bed and started dragging her towards the garden.

'He said I should never go looking for him, he said it can be dangerous!' Ranjana kept begging. But Giribala paid no heed to her entreaties.

'Don't come back if you can't keep your husband in your room.' She shut the door on her face.

The rest of the night Giribala stayed awake in her bed. She kept looking through her window. She could not see anything unusual. She finally fell asleep in the early hours of the morning and woke up to find the couple busy with their usual tasks. She never mentioned the night again, and they seemed to have forgotten the incident as well. She never saw the figure on the well again and, to Giribala's astonishment, her son seemed happy and taken in with Ranjana finally.

One night, she saw Ranjana from her window again, breaking her sankha on the walls of the well and laughing hysterically. Giribala ran downstairs, sweating with fear. When she opened the door to her son's room, she saw Rajeev lying in the bed, a slim veiled figure sitting astride him. The shankhchunni was slowly strangling him. His eyes were popping out. The ghost turned her head towards Giribala, got out of the bed, and crawled across the floor, leaving a trail of blood behind her. Two burning eyes stared at her from beneath the veil. The sankha on her hand made scratching noises on the floor.

Characteristics of the shankhchunni

- A skeletal, dark female ghost.
- Encounters with it can be fatal.
- Kills its victims painfully.
- When a married Hindu woman dies when her husband is still alive, she becomes this ghost.
- Seeks revenge on those who had anything to do with their death.
- Found in Bengal.

72

SHAYEED

Dalveer was looking at the horizon, a distant look in his eyes, while Nazma rested her head on his shoulder. Their grandfathers had fought side-by-side in a battle that had become part of village lore. This might have been part of the reason for their love for each other across the religious divide, but in the polarized country they lived in today, the fact that he was Hindu and she, a Muslim, meant that their love had to remain hidden. So, they devised ingenious ways to meet each other. People from the Hindu part of the village would not go near the Muslim quarter and vice versa. Dalveer knew Nazma would be ready for marriage soon and he became desperate to meet her as often as possible, to see if they could find a way out of this predicament.

'I don't know, Dalveer, this is risky. What if people saw us?'

'The cows ran away, what could I do if they came running to this place where I bumped into you?' Dalveer laughed.

He usually took his herd of cows to graze in the field behind the village. He knew he could always make excuses of cows running free from his control if anybody asked him. For a while the place was deserted, and nobody bothered their few moments of cherishing each other.

He came home with the same bittersweet feelings that he always had after seeing Nazma. He didn't know what made them have such strong feelings for each other. The mere thought of her getting married to someone else made his chest hurt. He spent the afternoon lost in thoughts of her. Around evening however, his father, Daljit, came to him, deeply distressed. He shouted:

'What have you done with the cows?'

'What do you mean?'

'They are not eating anything and shaking their head as if in pain!'

Nobody had been seriously worried until the cows started vomiting. Some of the village elders who were very worried by now asked Daljit where he had taken the herd for grazing. Daljit went looking for his son and found him in a corner of the house. His eyes were red, and his head was shaking madly. Daljit felt a chill in his stomach as he spotted the similarities with the malaise that had affected the cows. They called the local doctor, but he couldn't diagnose what had afflicted Dalveer or the cows. The hospital was too far away and Dalveer didn't look like he'd make it. One of the old men took Daljit aside.

'He must have been lurking around the back of the Muslim locality. A shayeed never fails to mark its presence. You should have told your son to stay away and follow the rules, Daljit. Neither he nor the cows can be saved now.'

Daljit lost his mind. He couldn't believe that he was losing his son as well as his entire herd of cows. He spent the night beside his son who started vomiting again around the morning.

Losing hope, the next day Daljit went running to the Muslim area to consult the resident pir. On his way to the pir's house, he saw a beautiful girl sitting under a tree. To his surprise, he found himself asking her about him.

'Did you see a young man in this area yesterday with a herd of cows? Do you know what's wrong with him?' Daljit asked helplessly.

'W-why? What's wrong with him?' Nazma could feel her heart pumping very fast.

'Well, he is about to die. Do you know what's a shayeed?'

Nazma felt her knees give way. Of course, she knew what a shayeed was. She had lost her uncle and a whole herd of goats to this terrible ghost that they had to keep away by performing some rituals mandated by a pir.

'I know what a shayeed is and how to save people from it. You need to bring your son to the pir, and he will be able to help you.'

'But we are Hindu. Are you sure this is going to work?'

'Ghosts have no religion!'

The whole village came to the purification ceremony of Daljit. As he was brought around, barriers were brought down as people from both religions prayed together to get rid of the evil.

Dalveer and Nazma were not sure whether it was love or evil that played the most significant role in eliminating hate from humanity. They still hoped to get married someday.

Characteristics of the shayeed
- A deadly spirit. Attacks humans and cattle.
- The ghost of a person who has died in battle.
- Found in Punjab.

73

SHEEKOL BURI

On calm afternoons in broad daylight, when nobody suspects anything could be lurking under the blue water of the ponds, the sheekol buri smiles in sheer joy. She waits with her long arms for unsuspecting swimmers to fall into her trap.

The sheekol buri or jol pisachi is the spirit of a woman who has drowned while still having unsatisfied desires; it, therefore, seeks to avenge itself against those it holds responsible for its fate. Often, the sheekol buri are the spirits of women who have committed suicide by drowning after suffering severe abuse from their much-older husbands and lovers. Some might have been murdered by being drowned by their lovers after an unwanted pregnancy. After their deaths, the spirits of those women continue to stay on earth, seeking vengeance. They have long hair, always wet as they live under water and their eyes do not have an iris. Sometimes, the sheekol buri can be seen in the dead of night sitting on trees but mostly they live under water.

She lures men to the middle of the pond or the river, binds

their legs with her long, tangled hair and then pulls them down to the same fate she was subjected to. Sometimes, she takes a human form and makes love to her victims and makes them swear vows of eternal love to her. If the men fail to keep their promise, she will resume her true form and drag them to the bottom of the river.

There are some possible explanations for the existence of these mythological creatures. First, the existence of sheekol buri could be seen as an example of the dire fate that could befall men who abuse and murder women. The legend of the sheekol buri might have also arisen as a warning to much older men preying on young women.

Characteristics of the sheekol buri

- A vengeful female spirit.
- Found in ponds and lakes.
- Encounters with it are fatal.
- Found in Bengal.

74

SILA

Sila or Si'la is a kind of supernatural female creature that existed in pre-Islamic Arabia. In Arabian culture, witches or hags are considered to be silas. They are sometimes associated with genies, and sometimes with ghouls.

Silas reside in the desert, in uninhabited, dark places. They take the form of attractive women who seduce men. These creatures lure travellers and nomads into their habitations and kill them. The silas can mate with humans and carry their children. They are also said to have sexual intercourse with sleeping men.

It is often believed that gemstones and enchanted pendants can protect someone from the effects of the sila.

Characteristics of the sila
- A female spirit with its origin in Arabian culture from where it spread to India.
- Encounters with it can be fatal.
- Resides in deserts and sparsely inhabited areas.

75

SKONDHOKATA

Evening descends with a subtle harmony in small towns. The buildings in which railway employees lived were situated by the side of the tracks and their residents timed their routines according to the passage of the trains. Papai's tuitions would begin when the evening Rajdhani Express passed by. Papai always double-checked his tasks before the doorbell rang. He wasn't sure if he entirely liked his new private tutor, Tanumoy. But the man was good at teaching, and Papai's mathematical skills had improved significantly after a few classes, even though Tanumoy's reserved mien and strange physical appearance intimidated Papai. A tall, thin man, he had a slightly larger-than-average head and spondylitis which caused him to wear a collar at all times.

Apart from scolding Papai occasionally for his poor math skills, Tanumoy was a good teacher. They talked about many things outside of studies. Tanumoy asked his student about school and his extended family. But Papai avoided talking about his family. After classes, Tanumoy sometimes chatted with Papai's mother about him. Papai liked that Tanumoy never complained about him to his mother. Only once had he broken that rule when Papai spilled water on him by mistake, which made him furious. Tanumoy got so angry that he almost strangled Papai. When he started choking, he let him go and said, 'You have a very small head,' and left.

Papai was shaken to the core. That day he did what he normally was prone to doing whenever he was depressed. He went up to the rooftop to watch the passing trains on the rail tracks beside their apartment building. That evening, after the Intercity Express passed with the usual loud rattling noise, the whole area subsided into silence. In the dim moonlight, he saw the tall figure of Tanumoy with his slightly large head and collar walking slowly through the rail track. He had said once he lived somewhere on the other side of the town, so perhaps he was walking home. Although he had been shaken by the incident, he decided he wouldn't tell his mother and would apologize to the irritable tutor—he realized this was because he had grown quite attached to Tanumoy.

But the tutor didn't come the next day. Papai waited eagerly for the doorbell to ring but it never rang. He kept asking his mother, but she said that the contact number that Tanumoy had provided was unserviceable. From that day onwards, he never showed up. Heartbroken, Papai would look for him on the streets on the way to school, trying to spot the familiar face. When the new conductor took over the duties of their school bus with a collar on his neck, oddly enough, he found himself drawn to the man; perhaps he saw something of Tanumoy in him. Every day after school, he was the first person to board the bus and spent the entire journey chatting with the conductor. The man too seemed to grow fond of Papai. After a few months he said he needed to change his job and leave town. Papai invited him to their house. His mother, slightly surprised at this unexpected attachment, nevertheless welcomed the bus conductor.

Papai spent the whole evening chatting with the bus conductor. He didn't understand why he felt so familiar. He even started talking about his father, a topic he always avoided. Almost a year ago his father had got run over by a train while on duty as a signalman. As a compensation, his mother had been given a job in the railway. Talking to this man, Papai felt a sharp twinge in his chest. He realized how much he missed his father and couldn't hold back tears any longer. The conductor held him in his long arms as Papai wept silently. To reassure Papai, he promised to stay in touch before leaving.

That night the moonlight felt warm and soothing. Papai went to the rooftop. The rail tracks were glistening like silver strings across dimly lit meadows. Once again, Papai spotted the familiar tall figure standing still on the rail track. But this time, the figure was holding his collar in his hand and there appeared to be no head on his shoulders. In his bones, Papai knew it would take his father a while to find a new head.

Characteristics of the skondhokata
- Has a human body with no head.
- If somebody is run over by a train, can become this spirit.
- Encounter with it can be fatal.
- Found mostly in West Bengal.

76

SUCCUBUS

The succubus and incubus are the female and male forms of a supernatural entity that is based on human–monster sexual fantasies. By definition, succubus is a female demonic creature that makes men succumb to its sexual fantasies. The word 'succubus' is derived from the Latin word 'succubare' which literally translates as 'to lie under', implying the sexual position wherein the man lies under the woman. Their origins can be traced to medieval legends and epics. In modern references, succubus is not always considered to be a demonic creature that appears in dreams but is sometimes used to refer to enchantresses or sexually alluring women.

All religious scriptures forbid sexual congress with the succubus. Anyone who enjoys sex with a succubus will die either immediately or slowly and painfully. Performing cunnilingus on a succubus is supposed to be especially dangerous.

The idea of the succubus is sometimes used to provide an explanation of those who suffer from 'sleep paralysis'. These creatures appear in the subconscious of the victims, especially if they are in the grip of dark sexual fantasies and causes them to freeze in fear.

Characteristics of the succubus

- Female spirit.
- Kills by having sexual intercourse with its victim.
- Found all over India.

77

SUPURUS

Malati liked the musty smell of a closed room. Every time they came back from a holiday, although her husband advised against it, she would inhale the smell for a while before opening the windows. Her husband, Subal, would tell her that the smell rose from vapours that hadn't been able to escape from sealed off spaces. But today Malati didn't go through her usual routine; she sat silently on the sofa as Subal aired the house. Malati observed their daughter, Rima, going to her bedroom and gently shutting the door. She wondered how long it would take for all of them to get over the abruptness of the incident.

Maybe everyone who had attended the sacred thread ceremony of Malati's nephew felt the same way right now. Watching a fifteen-year-old boy die right before their eyes would traumatize anyone. On top of that, it had taken place during the boy's own thread ceremony. After shaving off his hair, while coming down to the ground floor, his leg had got tangled in the long cloth dhoti he was wearing and he tripped and fell down the stairs. He had bled to death before help could arrive.

Everybody decided to return to their own homes to give the devastated family some time for themselves. But Rima hadn't wanted to leave. She had been very close to her cousin and the shock of his death hit her really hard. She didn't say a word on their way back. Even after arriving home, she locked herself in her own room. Only during the afternoon did she go to the rooftop. She loved being on the roof. Malati hoped that might make her feel better. When she still didn't come down by nightfall, Subal started to worry. Malati was on her way to the rooftop when she saw her daughter coming down the stairs. Rima glanced at her mother with bloodshot eyes and went straight to her room.

Malati was slightly worried. She knew her daughter had been crying a lot, but her eyes hadn't looked normal. She told Subal about this and they went to their daughter's room. Rima was lying on the bed talking to herself.

'You can't eat anything…. I won't wear a sari on the first day of college…no one will see….'

It didn't make any sense. Malati walked across the room and touched Rima's head. It was burning with fever. They knew it was due to the shock of recent events. After Subal gave her a dose of paracetamol, Malati tried to wash her head with cold water, when Rima suddenly sat up on her bed and started shouting: 'Get off me! I told you! Don't you dare touch me again!'

Feeling distraught, Malati and Subal called their family doctor. When he came over, Rima was still shouting and thrashing about on her bed as her parents tried to calm her down. The doctor felt worried and gave her a potent sedative. Within half an hour, she fell asleep and her temperature came down soon after, which was a relief for everyone.

Malati and Subal discussed the matter until late that night. Subal fell asleep but Malati couldn't. She felt like checking on Rima but restrained herself from going to her room for fear of disturbing her sleep. The medicine should work for at least twelve hours, but after the rough last few days, she felt deeply worried. Sighing, she closed her eyes.

Just then, she heard a soft noise from Rima's room. Like something was moving on the bed. Rima wasn't supposed to wake up all night. Malati hurried towards Rima's room. The door was closed, even though Malati clearly remembered keeping it ajar. She put an ear to the door. Somebody was definitely moving on the bed. She gently opened the door and looked in.

Rima was awake with her eyes wide open. A bloodless, pale, naked body was on top of her. It had a bald head and a huge mouth with which it was chewing on her daughter's face.

Characteristics of the supurus

- Teenage male ghost. When teenaged Brahmin boys die during their thread ceremonies, they turn into this ghost.
- Attacks young girls.
- Victims suffer from high fever and hallucinations.
- Can kill their victims.
- Found in West Bengal.

78

TOLA

'I've always wanted to become a painter,' Bapi said, looking at the watercolour painting his friend had made

Rana said, 'Then you will be!'

'You are so talented, Rana!'

Rana smiled.

The afternoon breeze played with their hair as they sat engrossed in painting the scene spread out in front of them. Rana knew this old building well. Bapi had been scared as they made their way up the rickety stairs to the rooftop, but when they got there, his fears melted away, the view was so spectacular. He often wondered what his friends from the city would think if they knew such a beautiful place existed not very far from Kolkata.

His friendship with Rana had started in the most unlikely fashion. When he had first arrived in this village a few weeks ago, to stay in seclusion in his grandparents' house in preparation for his sacred thread ceremony, he had been bored out of his mind. He had tried his hand at painting but even that had begun to fail after a couple of days. He had taken to wandering around the village all afternoon even though his grandfather had forbidden him from going outside.

One day, in the course of his wandering, Bapi fell into the river. The cliff he had been standing on crumbled under his feet and he was pitched into the water. When he opened his eyes underwater, briefly, he found himself looking into the kind face of a boy of about the same age as him. The stranger pulled him to the shore and introduced himself as Rana. From that moment onwards, besides saving him from drowning, Rana saved him from boredom as well.

Bapi wished Rana could come into the house so they could spend more time with each other. But that meant his secret adventures would be discovered by everyone. So, they only met in the afternoons and Bapi waited for those precious hours all day long. Rana also showed him his house beside the old temple at the edge of the village, along with all the secret interesting places. However, the rooftop of the ruined house was their favourite haunt once they discovered their common love for painting.

Finally, the day of Bapi's ceremony arrived. Bapi told Rana their family was invited to the occasion. Bapi was excited that he could finally show off his friend to everyone. He was extremely occupied with the rituals from the morning but kept an eye open for the people arriving to greet him. As part of the rituals, he'd have to isolate in a room for three days. He waited impatiently for the self-isolation to end. On the fourth day, a grand ceremony was held, which was attended by the entire village. Late that evening, his grandfather, accompanied by an old couple, came to meet him and introduced them as Mr and Mrs Banerjee, the family who lived in the house by the old temple. To Bapi's utter disappointment, Rana wasn't with them.

'Where is the rest of the family?' he asked.

Though slightly taken aback, they answered. 'This is our whole family, child.'

Mr Banerjee patted his head and Mrs Banerjee gave a wan smile. They left soon after.

Bapi waited the whole night impatiently. They were supposed to leave the village the next day; how could Rana betray him like this? Next morning, without waiting for anybody's permission, he headed straight to the house Rana had showed him. The couple from the previous night, surprised to see him, greeted him politely. Bapi didn't know how to ask who he was looking for and pretended to look around the house.

He was jolted to see the picture of a boy hanging on one of their walls. It was undoubtedly Rana's kind eyes looking at him.

'Who is he?' he asked, his heart racing wildly.

Mr Banerjee looked at the picture sadly.

'That was our son. Years ago, he died of drowning in the river. He too was awaiting his threading ceremony in a few days as well!'

Bapi froze to the spot. Mr Banerjee added: 'You know it's very unfortunate to die just before the threading ceremony. People are prone to accidents during those days and if the young boy passes away, their soul never gets a proper release. Our poor boy...I hope he found peace.'

Bapi felt his heart growing numb. He somehow managed to say: 'If his soul is not released, does that mean you can still see him sometimes?'

'I can't. I wish I was never threaded myself. Anybody who has been threaded can't see a lost soul.'

Bapi couldn't wait any longer. He knew where to find his friend. He ran for the old rooftop. The bright sunlight flooded the empty view. The river flowed peacefully below. Bapi felt an unbearable pain in his heart. The wind blew away his tears and played with his hair like always.

Characteristics of the tola

- The ghost of a boy.
- Helps people, likes to talk.
- When young boys die before their sacred thread ceremony, they turn into this ghost.
- Found in Bangalore.

79

ULKAMUKHI

A car decorated with flowers stopped in front of the Mukherjee mansion on a beautiful summer evening. Conches were blown and other auspicious rituals were performed to welcome the newlyweds. However, much of the celebrations was feigned because the wedding was a transaction—the wedding of the wealthy, middle-aged Pratap Mukherjee to the beautiful nineteen-year-old village bride, Shikha, was a grotesque occasion. The servants gossiped about it, and even the celebrations could barely disguise their disgust.

The Mukherjees had always been wealthy. But the senior Mukherjee had died while Pratap was still in school, and the family fortune had taken a bit of a beating because Pratap's doting mother did not curb any of his excesses or immoderate spending. Nevertheless, the family had been replenished by a vast amount of wealth after Pratap married a wealthy bride who had perished in a tragic accident a few years after they were married.

His new marriage wasn't something he'd wanted. A monstrous

womanizer, he had forced himself upon Shikha when his eye had been arrested by her beauty during an excursion to the village he owned. But if Pratap had thought he was going to get away with his assault of yet another village girl he was mistaken. This time the villagers arrived at his mansion with the girl and a lawyer in tow and had told him that he would have to marry the woman he had forced himself on, or face very unpleasant consequences.

Left with no choice, he had agreed to the marriage. Fuming, once they were inside his house, Pratap Mukherjee had locked himself in with his mother—the only person who sympathized with his troubles.

Shikha had been devastated after the night when Pratap Mukherjee had forced himself on her. She had thought of ending her life many times, especially when she discovered that she was pregnant with his child, but that would mean the scoundrel would get away with his sins. However, her father, who was a bold man, rallied the villagers to confront Mukherjee. As she now walked around the big house of the Mukherjee estate, she felt some satisfaction of having won a lost battle. Despite the heart-breaking reality of being married to her assailant, she was somewhat satisfied that these riches would belong to her child one day.

Pratap Mukherjee came out of his mother's room around nightfall after devising a careful plan. They couldn't bear the idea of this low-caste woman behaving like the empress of their estate or of her child gaining heirdom. Since legally, she could claim the property for Pratap's unborn child, the best solution was to get rid of her.

When he entered his bedroom at night, the bride was sitting on the bed with her veil drawn on her face. He felt a wave of

mirth bubbling inside at the audacity of this woman dressed up as a bride. He knew what he had to do. Closing the windows, he walked closer to her and asked: 'Did you think it would be this easy? You and your devious village? Did you think humiliating the Mukherjee family would have no consequences?'

She remained silent, so he continued. 'Many have tried to bring us down. We have been holding up this empire for a century and your low-caste child can never be a part of this.'

He held up a bottle of kerosene in his hand. 'Take off your veil. Let me have one last look at the face that thought it could dupe Pratap Mukherjee.'

The woman slowly unveiled her face. Pratap Mukherjee shrieked. Losing balance, he staggered and fell against the wall. He could still recognize that half-burnt face.

'You...but how? Y-you died, right in this room!'

The woman smiled at him.

'Indeed. You and your mother planned the secret marriage for my family fortune and after my father signed over his property, you burnt me alive here. Your mother would never allow another woman in your life, would she? Did you think you could repeat the same performance with another girl?'

'W-what do you want?' he stammered.

'The girl and her child will own this property after your death.' She moved close to him. 'You are not going to destroy any more lives, Pratap Mukherjee.'

While saying so, she opened her mouth. A wave of fire jetted out and engulfed the kerosene bottle which exploded in Pratap's face. He died a painful death.

In the next room, Shikha woke up because of the ruckus. She

hadn't bothered going to Pratap Mukherjee's bedroom and instead had decided to sleep in a separate room. In the darkness, she spotted a lady dressed in bridal attire pause beside her window. She smiled sadly at Shikha and gradually melted into the pale moonlight.

Characteristics of the ulkamukhi

- A female ghost.
- When she opens her mouth, flame shoots out of it.
- If a woman is burnt alive, she becomes an ulkamukhi.
- Encounters with it can be fatal.
- Found in Bengal.

80

VETALA

The idea of a phantom being that can bring dead bodies to life, or turn them into semi-living moving spectres, is a frightful thought. Although the betal or vetala has never been portrayed as a particularly scary creature, it is believed to bring dead people back to life to do its bidding. The vetala is considered a wise being that also dwells in charnel houses and burial grounds. He can possess dead bodies and leave them at his will. According to Hindu mythology, when a young virgin boy with immense knowledge is sacrificed or murdered, he turns into a vetala. Though they have the power to control the dead, they have never been heard of causing harm to living beings.

If anyone gains control over a vetala, it can be used to fulfil wishes. If ill-intentioned, the controller can coerce the vetalas into doing heinous deeds.

The most explicit descriptions of the vetala are in Ishwar Chandra Vidyasagar's *Betal Panchabinsati* stories, where the relationship between a vetala and the wise king Vikramaditya was

established. The king promises a tantric that he will capture a vetala and bring it to him for fulfilling his wishes. The vetala, a wise old spirit, enters into an agreement with King Vikramaditya, that involves him telling the king a story at the end of which would be a riddle that the king would have to answer. If the answer was correct, the vetala would return to the tree. But if the king failed to answer the riddle, vetala, as a captive, would be bound to ride on Vikramaditya's back to wherever he takes him. If the king knew the answer and didn't say it out loud, his head would split into pieces. The vetala told King Vikramaditya twenty-four stories that had a riddle at the end which the king had to answer. He knew the answers to all of them, and when he gave the correct answers to Vetala, the corpse flew off his shoulder back into the tree. The king then climbed back up and brought down the corpse, and, carrying it on his shoulder, began walking to the cremation ground. Then the vetala entered the body again and told the king another story. This was repeated twenty-four times until King Vikramaditya couldn't answer the twenty-fifth question and th vetala agreed to go with him to the tantrik. However, on their way to the tantrik, the vetala told his story to the king. He was one of the twin brothers promised to their parents by the tantrik, with a condition that the boys would be educated under his supervision. He had been given immense amount of knowledge while his brother would only learn the basics. Later on, the tantrik returned the brother to their parents and sacrificed him to make him a vetala for fulfilling his evil wishes and gain more power in the world of dark magic. He escaped from his captivity. Now the secret desire of the tantrik is to sacrifice the king, since he was another potential young soul with immense knowledge and could be become another vetala at his service. Equipped with this knowledge, the king killed the tantrik and set the vetala free. Satisfied with his kind deed, the vetala agreed to serve the king whenever he wished.

Characteristics of the vetala
- One of the most famous spirits in Hindu mythology.
- Found in crematoriums and burial grounds.
- Highly intelligent.

81

VIRAN

The word 'vire' or 'viran' means 'hero' in Tamil, and there are many spirits and statues and idols who have the term 'viran' or 'veeram' attached to them. The statues are often situated in the forests of Goddess Mariamman's temples and are expected to protect her.

In ancient times it was not uncommon for blood sacrifices to be made for the viran. Some of the better-known ones are the Madurai viran, Muniyandi viran, Muniyappa viran, and so on.

There are similar kinds of warrior spirits, to be found across the country, including the birs from Uttar Pradesh, and the kharbar, kera, and genda from Jaunpur and Nagpur.

Characteristics of the viran
- Warrior spirit.
- Can be dangerous to intruders.
- Found across India.

82

YAKSHA

Yakshas and yakshis are the male and female forms of a group of supernatural creatures in Hinduism, Jainism, and Buddhism. Usually known to be kind, they are associated with water, fertility, foliage, treasures, and the wilderness. Yakshas are usually benevolent, fairy-like creatures that one might run into in forests and mountains; however, there are also other kinds of yakshas who are demons and eat humans, especially travellers.

Yakshas are found in the sculptures of the Mauryan empire, ranging from third to first century BCE. Usually about 2 metres in height, surrounded by inscriptions, they are either represented as fearsome warriors or mean dwarfs. The yakshi statues all depict ethereal young women.

The god of wealth, Kubera, is considered as the king of all the yakshas. Draped with glittering jewellery, Kubera has a corpulent body and carries a pot of money and a club. He is often portrayed alongside the goddess of prosperity and wealth, Lakshmi.

In Buddhist beliefs, the yakshas protect righteous people instead of treasures. In Jain belief, the yakshas are just like other mortal beings, albeit with supernatural powers; they are born, reproduce, and die. Jain depictions represent the yaksha and yakshi together. There are twenty-four yakshas and yakshis each who serve as the shasan-devatas of the ruling/controlling gods for the twenty-four tirthankaras.

In literature, Kalidas portrayed the yaksha as a romantic hero, lamenting the loss of his beloved, but in the Mahabharata, in the dialogues of Yaksha Prashna, a yaksha in the form of a crane is found asking tricky questions to Yudhishthira as the Pandavas are at the end of their twelve-year exile. In Sri Lankan poems, yakshas are often found in the court's royalty and serving as loyal subjects to the House of Vijaya and the yaksha chief sat with the kings.

In popular Bengali folk tales like that of Thakumar Jhuli and such others, the yakshas protect hidden underground vaults of gold. If someone discovers them, they can only lay their hands on them if they are able to solve riddles posed by yaksha guardians.

Characteristics of the yaksha
- Supernatural beings with their origin in Hindu, Buddhist, Jain myth and folklore.
- Is usually kind but can occasionally be mean-spirited.
- Widely found across Asia.

83

YUGINI

The yugini is a deadly, grotesque supernatural creature. It falls into the category of petni among the ghosts described in Bengali folklores. The yugini can shape-shift into any human or animal form or can remain invisible to human eyes. It usually lurks around in deserted paddy fields under the scorching sun of a hot summer noon. If some unlucky wanderer strays in their path, they develop a high fever and begin speaking gibberish afterwards.

In their true form, yuginis are headless with eyes glowing from their breasts. They have also been described as middle-aged women with saggy breasts hanging down to the waist.

In Hindu mythology, the yugini serves as a maid to Goddess Shetala, the goddess of smallpox. It is believed that when an angry Shetala curses a village with a smallpox, these yuginis are sent down to spread the disease and are rewarded with a feast of the rotting bodies of those who succumb to the disease.

There are many religious ways to reverse the adverse effects of the spell of yuginis. The gunins, religious supernatural experts, would chant hymns to beg forgiveness of the yuginis or seek their blessings. In some traditions around the mountainous regions, people sacrifice black hens to gain favour with the yuginis.

Characteristics of the yugini

- A female spirit.
- Encounters with it are fatal.
- Found in Bengal.

84

ZOTING

'Ting!' Raima woke up with a jolt. With half-open eyes, she checked the time. It was 3 a.m. Before she put her phone on silent mode, she quickly checked the notifications on the screen. She saw an unread email from Zubair. For almost three weeks she had been waiting to hear from him. Sitting upright now, Raima felt the same excitement as she had felt on the day Zubair left for his new assignment. She started reading the email...

Dear Raima,

You were right. I should have emailed you earlier. But I was waiting for the right time. I know how you always say that sometimes time can go wrong. And you were right.

Do you remember the time when we were desperately looking for information about this mysterious village? How we kept getting lost! Well, the search hasn't been any easier. I was hoping that the email we received from that stranger would somehow help in getting to the source of the story. After I had arrived at the station on the southernmost coast of Maharashtra, I found out that our contact does not exist. For days, I searched for the address he had given but it was a wrong address. I was frustrated and often I was tempted to give up and return.

You once told me that when you search for something, you are actually being found. I decided to do one final search. I went to the market area and approached an old man who looked at me with great interest—perhaps, my misery caught his attention. When I asked him about the village I was looking for, he replied, 'All places that once existed will always exist. We can override the references, but places are immutable.'

There was something unsettling about his voice. This feeling of disquiet lingered about him, on to which the waves rolled unceasingly. I couldn't help following him after his work was finished. After taking a lot of wrong turns, we ended up on the seashore.

Do you remember when we visited that beautiful cliff-side beach? This beach had a similar setting. A calm, smooth surface of dark sands taking in the waves, and a high cliff marking the end of the beach. The man wandered away from me, and eventually knelt down on the sand, facing the cliff. From a distance, I watched his silent, kneeling silhouette against the magnificent sunset. After fidgeting for a while, I thought of leaving. Then he stood up, turned around, and walked back to where I was. Pointing to the other side of the cliff, he said, 'That is where they wait. That is what they always do.'

His words didn't make any sense. I went back to my hotel. Yet, I couldn't get him out of my head all night. Next morning, I walked to the other side of the cliff.

A sign that said 'Quarantine Zone' stood in front of a field. To my surprise nobody stopped me from going further. The more I progressed, the stranger it seemed. I entered what looked like a neat, orderly village with rows of huts, a market area, wells, schools, etc. Yet, there was not a single person in sight. It seemed like all of them had left in a hurry. The doors of the huts stood ajar, and the shops were filled with goods. I walked around all day. By the time, evening arrived, I realized that it was 'our' village— the one we had figured that had disappeared from the map.

Then I saw the first inhabitant of the village. A silent, headless figure was strolling along the side of the burial ground. I stood rooted to the spot. A few others followed the first figure. They seemed oblivious of my presence.

I tried to walk away but realized the whole place was now teeming with these headless, silent bodies strolling on the streets. Most of them gathered around the burial ground.

You were right, Raima. This is the village where a deadly disease broke out a few years ago. The fear of the unknown has always driven humans to bring out the deadliest demons within themselves. As the virus seemed unstoppable, people from nearby localities locked the whole village down. Nobody was allowed to get out of this place. Many died from the disease. Since then, they have kept strolling around the spot where they died.

Does that make you wonder how I found them concentrated around the burial ground? Well, they were buried alive, or burnt even before the disease could take them. The living wanted to get rid of the diseased without pity or mercy, so fearful were they of the pandemic. When the outside world shut the door on them they remained here forever.

I know about all these since I realized that once you come inside this place, you can never go out. This whole area is secluded forever. They wanted to be heard, so you did hear them without stepping into the 'Quarantine Zone'. By the time you get here, I will be one of them—a silent, headless form strolling on these streets. Abandoned.

You are right. It is quite late.

Zubair

Characteristics of the zoting

- Quiet, harmless ghosts strolling around the place where they died.
- Has a headless body with lean limbs and torso.
- When people from the Karvi or Koli castes or a person from the Muslim community dies an unnatural death, they become this ghost.
- Found in the Konkan area.

ACKNOWLEDGEMENTS

Everyone who walks by me every day, everyone who is no longer with us, everyone who taught me about life and everyone who encouraged me to look past death—all of them have played their part in the making of this book, not to mention everything I have been able to accomplish. I am thankful to my teachers, well-wishers, and everyone who has rooted for me. Words fail me when it comes to describing how grateful I am to my mother for her support. Not only did she help me with my writing and research, she was responsible for my overcoming of my fear of ghosts in the first place. As the world struggled with the pandemic, my constant source of support was Raka whose wonderful illustrations grace this book; she helped me with the writing of the stories as well. Both of us are grateful to members of our families for their support.

AUTHOR'S NOTE

Ghosts exist in every corner of the subcontinent, from the high Himalaya to the coast of Kanyakumari, from the Sundarbans to the slums of Dharavi. In the many years I have spent researching and studying the ghosts of India, I have found that some of my very best source material came from my fellow citizens of all ages and interests. They might have encountered denizens of the spirit world in their own lives, or in stories told by their grandmothers. The ghosts described in this book are only a small fraction of the phantoms to be found in our country. If any reader wants to share with me a story of ghosts that they have personally experienced, I'd be delighted to hear from you at the following email address: banerjeeriksundar@gmail.com

If they are included in a future edition of the book, full credit will be given to the source of the story and the contributor will receive a free copy of *The Book of Indian Ghosts*.

SELECT BIBLIOGRAPHY

'Papers on Applied Psyche-Analysis', Chapter 22, *The Uncanny*, 1919.

Aharter, Whitmore Edward, *The Supernatural in Modern English Fiction*, New York and London: G. P. Putnam's Sons, 1917.

Anderson, Laurie Halse, *Wintergirls*, New York: Penguin Books, 2009.

Blanco, Maria del Pilar and Peeren, Esther (ed.), *The Spectralities Reader: Ghosts and Haunting in Contemporary Cultural Theory*, London: Bloomsbury, 2013.

Cavendish, Richard, *The Powers of Evil in Western Religion, Magic and Folk Belief*, London: Routledge & Kegan Paul, 8 volumes, 1975.

Chatman, Seymour (ed.), *Literary Style: A Symposium*, London and New York: Oxford University Press, 1971.

————, *Story and Discourse: Narrative Structure in Fiction and Film*, Ithaca and London: Cornell University Press, 1978.

Crooke, William, *The Popular Religion and Folklore of Northern India*, Vol. 1, (originally published in 1986).

Foster, E. M., *Aspects of the Novel*, New York & London: Harcourt Brace Jovanovich, 1974.

Freud, Sigmund, *Collected Papers*, Vol. 4, London: The Hogarth Press and The Institute of Psycho-Analysis, 1925.

Genette, Gérard, *Narrative Discourse*, translated by Jane E. Lewin, New York: Cornell University Press, 1980.

Guiley, Rosemary Ellen, *The Encyclopedia of Ghosts and Spirits*, Checkmark Books, 2007.

Harland, Richard, *Super Structuralism: The Philosophy of Structuralism and Post-Structuralism*, London: Methuen, 1987.

Homer, *The Illiad*, London: Penguin Books, 1950.

Mike, Bal, *Narratology: Introduction to the theory of Narrative*, Toronto: University of Toronto Press, 1989.

Mill, J. S., *System of Logic*, New York: Harper & Brothers, 1843.

Mubarki, Meraj Ahmed, *Filming Horror Hindi Cinema: Ghosts and Ideologies*, Kolkata: SAGE, 2016.

Noel, Carroll, *The Philosophy of Horror or Paradoxes of the Heart*, London: Routledge, 1990.

Paul, Brunton, *Secret of Ancient Egypt*, UK: Arrow Books, 1965.

Penzoldt, Peter, *The Supernatural in Fiction*, Part 1, London: Peter Nevill, 1952.

Rimmon-Kenan, Shlomith, *Narrative Fiction: Contemporary Poetics*, London: Routledge, 1996.

Scarborough, Dorothy, *The Supernatural in Modern English Fiction*, New York and London: G. P. Putman's Sons, 1917.

Sen, Sukumar, *Golper Bhut*, Kolkata: Ananda Publishers, 2005 (third reprint).

Toolan, Michael J. (ed)., *The Stylistics of Fiction: A Literary-Linguistic Approach*, London and New York: Routledge, 1990.

Whitmore, Charles Edward, *The Supernatural in Tragedy*, Cambridge: Harvard University Press, 1915.